THE UNHINGED SERIES

More by Nicole Edwards

The Alluring Indulgence Series
Kaleb
Zane
Travis
Holidays with the Walker Brothers
Ethan
Braydon
Sawyer
Brendon

The Club Destiny Series
Conviction
Temptation
Addicted
Seduction
Infatuation
Captivated
Devotion
Perception
Entrusted

The Dead Heat Ranch Series
Boots Optional
Betting on Grace

The Devil's Bend Series
Chasing Dreams
Vanishing Dreams

Standalone Novels
A Million Tiny Pieces

Writing as Timberlyn Scott
Unhinged
Unraveling
Chaos

BOOK 1

The Unhinged Series

Nicole Edwards

Writing as **Timberlyn Scott**

SL Independent Publishing, LLC
PO Box 806
Hutto, Texas 78634
www.slipublishing.com

Unhinged, Book 1 – **An Unhinged Novel** is a work of fiction. Names, characters, businesses, places, events and incidents either are the products of the author's imagination or used in a fictitious manner. Any resemblance to actual persons, living or dead, business establishments, events, or locales is entirely coincidental.

Cover Image: © Artem Furman - Fotolia.com
Cover Design: © Nicole Edwards Limited

ISBN: 978-1-939786-31-9

Dear Reader,

I wanted to take a moment to introduce my writing style as Timberlyn Scott. Just so you're aware, if you're expecting the erotic elements that you are familiar with in my other series and standalone novels, you won't find that here. As Timberlyn Scott, I'm exploring a different aspect to my writing, including 1st person POV and a more contemporary/new adult feel. However, you will find a spicy love story. With that said, I hope you enjoy Sebastian and Payton's story.

Love,

Nicole

Dedication

This book is dedicated to
my husband, my daughter and my two boys.

Your unwavering support and pride in what I do humbles
me. Because of you, I strive to be better each and every day.

You are my heart, never forget that.

Contents

Prologue

I knew I was asleep. I had to be. Even knowing that, I was having a hard time deciphering the dream from reality. There was no way this could be real. Could it?

I didn't want to wake up. I didn't want to lose this moment.

This person, whoever they were, they mesmerized me, drew me in. I couldn't pull my eyes away, couldn't break the spell they had on me. Something in the way they walked, talked, moved.

Breathed.

So familiar, yet not.

I felt like I knew them, like I'd met them before, but for the life of me I don't remember any such encounter. Had we met? Was this my mind conjuring up the image of something from my past? Or was this some sort of vision from the future?

Either way, I didn't want to open my eyes. Didn't want to face reality if they weren't in it. I wanted to get closer, to look into their eyes, to know what they were thinking.

I was unabashedly staring, unable to look away.

Whoever this person was, there was something about them...

Something that unhinged me.

Chapter One

Payton
Monday morning

"Ms. Fowler, I'll never be able to stress enough how important this is," the domineering woman who stood just a few feet away, hands on her hips, head cocked to the side, said as she glared down at me. "Mr. Trovato's biggest pet peeve is his calendar."

I tried to pay attention, really. I was doing my best to jot down notes, but I'd recently learned — in the last hour and forty-seven minutes — that Jasmine Masters talked faster than anyone I knew. And based on what this woman told me, Mr. Trovato, the man I was now working for, was quite needy — at least in my humble opinion.

As much as I was trying to like Jasmine, the feat was rather difficult to do with a woman I'd met less than two hours ago. The same one who insisted on narrowing her blue eyes on me as though I was growing mold on the side of my face or something. Even once I got past her condescending tone and belittling stare, I still wasn't sure how she managed to sneak so many words into a single breath.

Maybe talking like punctuation wasn't in existence was one of the requirements of being an administrative assistant to the most-powerful man at Trovato, Inc., and if that were the case, I was beginning to wonder whether or not I was actually qualified for the job.

When a representative of Trovato, Inc. had called a few weeks ago to tell me that I'd passed the first series of aptitude tests and to come in for an interview, I had nearly passed out. I wasn't sure what to expect when I submitted my application, but without any other alternatives, I'd given it a shot. Now, I wasn't so sure I was going to fit in here.

"Every morning, you need to make sure you have his calendar printed and placed on his desk. He will also check and double check it on his phone. He gets here no later than six o'clock, so I suggest you get here at five."

I wondered if Mr. Trovato knew that his admin made him sound like an anal wack job. Who did that? Who studied their calendar like that? I didn't state the question aloud. After all, that wasn't my business. I'm sure I had a few quirks people didn't understand.

"He'll expect coffee and a briefing of what his day entails," Jasmine added before turning and walking away from me.

Where was she going now? I wondered as I took off after her.

"Briefing?" I realized just a second too late that I sounded like an idiot.

"Yes." Jasmine glanced back at me as though I was a third grader who had just screwed up reciting the alphabet. Then again, maybe I had. With so many instructions and rules running through my overloaded brain, I wasn't even sure whether today was still Monday or if we'd already moved on to Tuesday.

"When he arrives, make his coffee, give him ten minutes to get situated and then knock on his door," Jasmine instructed as she retrieved a sheet of paper from the printer before thrusting it in my direction.

I skimmed the page, unable to read the fine print, but I did clearly see the title: HOW TO MAKE COFFEE.

Awesome. I could hardly make coffee for myself and now I had the responsibility of making it for someone else. The day just kept getting better.

"Once he invites you in, you'll go over his meetings for the day," Jasmine continued. "Be sure to tell him who he's meeting with and when, whether or not he'll be taking a call or if he's expected to be somewhere."

Wouldn't he already know this if he studied his calendar three times?

Rather than ask that, I nodded. "Are most of them calls?" I waited for Jasmine to answer while I wondered just how this all worked. Since the extent of my job history was as a billing assistant at a small computer company and the little bit of time I'd worked at my dad's body shop, I just didn't know.

"Not usually, although he'll have plenty of them. Most of the time he'll meet with people in his office."

I would too if I had an office like his. The place was the size of a starter home and that made me wonder just what kind of pompous asshole I was going to be dealing with. I mean seriously. The building wasn't all that big to begin with, but that office… it was roughly the size of the warehouse area downstairs.

"If he has a trip coming up, make sure you remind him every day until the day before," Jasmine continued, evidently oblivious to my internal thoughts. "Getting his itinerary right is crucial. Make sure everything's in order, flight information, car service, hotel, dinner reservations. And if you screw that up, he'll make you come along on future trips so you can suffer right along with him."

Come along? Oh, no. No way. I certainly wasn't signing up to travel that was for sure.

"But that should be easy for you," Jasmine commented snidely.

What should be easy for me? I was lost for a moment, staring back at Jasmine. Was she saying that I wasn't capable of handling this job? Did she doubt me, too? Or was that just me?

I didn't get to ask any questions because Jasmine tacked on, "I'm sure you know what I'm talking about."

No, actually, I was completely lost, thank you very much.

My head was spinning and I was already convincing myself that I would screw this up. I possibly already had based on the way Jasmine was scowling at me.

"Come on, girl, you can do this, right?" Jasmine pinned me with her sapphire eyes.

I was pretty sure those were contacts, but I wasn't getting close enough to find out, mainly because Jasmine never stopped moving.

Focus, Payton.

"Sure," I lied, trying to sound confident. I'd been an assistant before, so surely I could figure this out. It wasn't rocket science. I mean how freaking hard could it be to manage someone's calendar and to bring him coffee every morning?

I got the distinct impression that those were just two of the millions of things I would have to do as Mr. Trovato's assistant. The only frame of reference I had where the job was concerned was my father's shop. I'd been his assistant for a short period of time, but since he owned a small body shop with roughly ten employees, it really wasn't the same thing. Jasmine had kindly informed me that Trovato, Inc. had somewhere around two hundred employees.

Yep. That's like… one hundred times two.

That might not sound like a lot, but to me, it was.

Jasmine placed her hands on her slender hips and faced off with me once more. Not wanting to appear any more incompetent than I already had, I squared my shoulders and looked up at the woman. She made me feel as though I were two feet tall and that didn't have anything to do with the fact that I was short either.

I fought the urge to squirm in the ill-fitting business suit I was wearing. Although it was supposed to be a power suit, it didn't help me feel at all powerful when I was greeted by Jasmine, who was wearing a pair of designer jeans and a colorful blouse, her auburn hair severely pulled back in a ponytail. I figured the woman was in her mid-thirties, but she looked all of eighteen dressed like that.

Since I hadn't seen anyone other than the gray-haired receptionist who greeted me at the main entrance — and she was sitting behind a desk — I really wasn't sure what the dress code actually was around this place. *Was it different for me because I was new? Or did everyone wear casual wear to the office on Monday?*

As I fought the urge to scratch beneath the itchy polyester blend, I prayed someone would tell me. I wasn't looking forward to dressing up tomorrow, not to mention, I really wasn't sure what else I had to wear. I'd spent a pretty penny on this stupid suit, along with another one that I'd worn to the interview three weeks ago.

"What time did I say he gets here?" Jasmine asked, her snootiness dragging me out of my thoughts, forcing me to forget about what was hanging in my closet in my tiny little apartment.

Refusing to look down at my notes, it took me a second to scan my memory. I had to mentally flip past the few pairs of jeans in my closet before it came to me. "Six," I stated uncertainly.

"Good."

I was tempted to stick my tongue out at her, feeling incredibly childish and a tad rebellious. I wasn't sure what it was about me that made this woman want to look down her narrow nose, but it was really beginning to grate on my nerves.

Jasmine laughed haughtily, at what, I don't know. I don't think I stuck my tongue out, but hell, maybe I did.

"And what time will *you* be here?" she asked, her arms crossing over her chest, as though she figured I surely couldn't answer two questions in a row.

"Five," I stated more affirmatively. Although I sounded somewhat sure, I was already trying to figure out just how I was going to drag my ass out of bed that early in the morning. As it was, getting here at eight that morning had been hard enough. But to be there by five, I was going to have to get up at… three. *Oh, crap.* I fought the urge to hang my head in defeat.

When I had originally applied for the job, I admit that I hadn't paid any attention to where Trovato, Inc. was located. I'd Googled the address for the interview only to find that the company had recently moved. Rather than their previous location near downtown Austin, they had moved to be more centrally located to the Circuit of the Americas. Since the new Formula One race track had been constructed south of the Austin airport that put me, oh, like an hour away. Okay, maybe not that far, but it was at least a forty minute drive and that was if I took the toll road. The idea of paying for tolls didn't sit well with me, especially when money was tight at the moment. But then again… a few dollars for an extra half hour of sleep. Hmm.

The job was paying well, so maybe I could work that into my budget.

Jasmine leaned over her desk, placing her perfectly manicured hands flat on the top as she stared back at me. When she began to tap one fingernail repeatedly, I realized she was waiting for me to say something.

Oops. I think I'd gotten lost in my own head again.

Rather than answer, I got distracted by the little design on her fingernail.

Note to self: this weekend get a manicure and have highlights touched up.

Yeah, it was safe to say that even wearing this uncomfortable blue suit, by comparison I still probably looked like a slob although I was the one dressed up. Where Jasmine's chestnut hair was pulled back in a ponytail, not a single hair out of place, my waist length brown hair was loose, not to mention frizzy, thanks to the humidity. I hadn't bothered to curl it, something I knew helped me look not quite so young, because I'd been out of time. Thanks to my alarm clock. Well, technically it was the snooze button's fault. If there wasn't a snooze button, I probably wouldn't have hit it five times. As a result, I'd been running late on my first day.

"There's no option for failure here, girl. He'll eat you alive if you don't get it right."

"Don't listen to her," a rumbling voice sounded from behind me.

My heart kicked into high gear, mimicking the way it beat when I attempted to work out at the gym. *Attempted* being the key word there. I was pretty sure I looked like a floundering hog when I struggled to run on the treadmill.

Hoping whoever was behind me didn't realize I was startled, or thinking about floundering hogs, I spun around to face him.

Oh, wow. He was… so not what I expected to see attached to that deep, booming voice.

If I thought Jasmine was tall, well, this man made the other woman look petite by comparison. It didn't help that I barely topped five feet, although my driver's license read five-two, thanks to a little fudging on my part. Aside from towering over me, the man was nicely dressed, clean shaven, with thick eyebrows hovering low over piercing brown eyes.

"And you are?" he asked, his voice reflecting the authority I was pretty sure he brandished.

I glanced down to see his hand — also well-manicured — as he held it out to me, I tried to remember why I was there. Pure instinct had me reaching out to take the proffered hand as I said, "Payton Fowler."

His grip was firm, confident. His skin strangely soft.

Manicure. Right.

"Nice to meet you, Payton Fowler. I'll call you Payton if you don't mind."

I shook my head. "I… uh… No, sir, I don't mind."

"Good. And you can call me Conrad."

I nodded, trying to figure out where I'd heard that name. Conrad… Conrad…

Oh, for heaven's sake, there was no doubt about it. I was screwing it all up.

I was in the process of shaking the hand of the founder and CEO of Trovato, Inc., Conrad Trovato himself.

With a name like Trovato, I had assumed Italian. Don't ask me why. But this guy didn't resemble any Italian guy I knew. Not that I knew many.

If any.

Okay, so that didn't matter.

When he glanced down at our joined hands, I realized I had latched on, and he was in the process of trying to pull away, but I wasn't letting him go. I was too busy staring at him, trying to remember why I'd agreed to take this job. What had made me think I was capable of being an administrative assistant to a self-made billionaire in the first place?

Someone cleared their throat and I wasn't sure whether it was Mr. Trovato or Jasmine. At the moment, their voices sounded eerily the same. But either way, I pulled myself together and released his hand, meeting his formidable gaze.

"I'll be meeting my wife for lunch today. Ensure we have reservations at eleven."

Yeah. Okay. So he was talking to me. I knew I should have uttered something smart, but for the life of me, I couldn't remember what he'd just said. The powerful aura that radiated off the man had paralyzed my brain, making me worthless.

"Yes, Mr. Trovato." Jasmine's throaty chuckle sounded way too fake.

"She'll do fine."

Conrad obviously was *not* talking to me. Thank God.

I wanted to ask him how he knew that. Maybe he'd enlighten me because I definitely didn't feel like I was going to do fine.

"We'll get the reservations taken care of immediately," Jasmine assured him, smiling.

Conrad nodded his head, turned and walked toward the office that spanned the north side of the building, closing his door behind him. Jasmine had given me a fleeting view of that room when I arrived. Other than noting its ridiculous size, a glimpse of the floor to ceiling windows lining the entire north wall, the grand walnut desk that sat in the middle of the room and the row of bookshelves on one side was the extent of my tour. I do remember thinking that that one single space was probably larger than the three bedroom apartment I shared with my two closest friends.

I stared after Conrad. He was distinguished, some would probably even say handsome. For an old man. Err… Old*er*. I didn't know exactly how old he was, but the crown of perfectly styled gray hair led me to believe he was older.

"You're gonna have to do better than that, girl," Jasmine whispered, her smile falling.

"He's so…" *Do not say old. Do not say old.* "Intimidating." I wasn't even aware I had spoken aloud until Jasmine snorted with laughter. Until then, I was beginning to wonder whether she knew how, and now the rusty sound echoed through the open reception area of the second floor.

My floor.

Technically the floor belonged to Mr. Trovato, but aside from his office, the only other occupied space was an area where my desk was positioned and a small section that contained a fancy leather sofa for clients to wait for Mr. Trovato. There were windows everywhere, providing enough natural light to light up the entire space, and that was without the help of the dangling fluorescent bulbs from above.

A miniscule kitchenette, equipped with a refrigerator, sink, and an industrial coffeemaker was tucked into a nook in one corner; a place Jasmine told me would be essential for me to learn my way around since Mr. Trovato loved his coffee more than he loved his family.

I was pretty sure she'd been joking about that last part.

"That's an understatement, girl. Now, let's continue. I'm only here for two more days and I suggest you pull it together or you're gonna be looking for another job."

No, not that.

At twenty-three, I had spent the last seventeen months looking for a job, coming up empty except for the occasional temp placement. It had been more than a year since I had graduated from college with big dreams and even bigger expectations. As it turned out, there was something like forty percent of people in Austin, Texas who had a bachelor's degree or higher, which meant that businesses could be as particular as they wanted to be in hiring.

That was something that would have been beneficial to learn in college. *Before* I picked a major.

With a degree in English Literature, I wasn't having much luck finding a job in a city that was dominated by tech companies. But three weeks ago, my dad had stumbled upon an ad on the internet for an administrative assistant position at Trovato, Inc. Of course, my father knew everything there was to know about the company that manufactured performance engines because he made it his business to stay up to date on the ins and outs of the automotive industry.

Not exactly the place I saw myself working for my first real job out of college, but now that I was here, I had to admit it wasn't quite as bad as I'd expected.

From the instant I stepped through the main doors, I'd been in awe of the place. Glass and steel constructed the building, and there were actually engines that decorated the space.

Engines. Like the things that went in cars.

The walls were white, the floor slate gray and the décor interesting.

It went without saying that those engines — or the components within them, I wasn't quite sure — had made Mr. Trovato rich.

When I arrived that morning, I hadn't had a lot of time to admire the unusual decorations. As I had attempted to ascend the stairs to the second floor, I was nearly tackled by a big, beefy security guard, who defended the stairs as though they led to heaven and I hadn't yet been permitted to pass the pearly gates.

"Earth to Payton."

I blinked twice, looking up at Jasmine.

"Two days, remember?" Jasmine nodded her head toward the notebook in my hand. "You might want to start writing. It's gonna be a long day for you."

I had a feeling that Jasmine was full of understatements. And her crash course in managing Mr. Trovato's calendar was just beginning.

Chapter Two

Payton
Monday night

By the time I walked to my car in the deserted parking lot, it was after seven, the sun had long since gone down and I was starving. Mr. Trovato was apparently an early riser and he had a penchant for staying at the office late, which didn't do anything to help the fact that I hadn't brought my lunch with me — something I had realized after my stomach started rumbling.

While Jasmine had gone out with some of her friends (in case there was any doubt, *no*, I wasn't invited), I had sat at the desk and pretended to munch on an invisible granola bar although no one was there to talk to me about the nutritional value in the pretend meal.

Didn't help that I had spotted a vending machine on the main floor — *just now* — on my way out the door.

During the two hours it took for Jasmine to celebrate her recent engagement and upcoming relocation to New York, I had fielded at least thirty phone calls. Thirty freaking calls.

I'm pretty sure Jasmine was on the verge of a heart attack when she came back and tried to make sense of the mess that I'd made with that little pink message pad. Luckily, it hadn't taken that long to sort out, but we — translated to *she*, because I don't think she trusted me at that point — spent the better part of the afternoon calling people back and scheduling meetings for Mr. Trovato.

Now, as I approached my car, my feet were hurting, my head was pounding and my eyes were slowly but surely drifting closed. I was exhausted and part of me was dreading coming back tomorrow.

Forcing the thought of what tomorrow might bring out of my throbbing head, I climbed into my car — a vintage, carbon steel gray, 1965 fastback Mustang that my father insisted I drive — and cursed the idea of having to look at a computer screen or a telephone ever again.

Speaking of telephones…

My cell phone sang *Baby Got Back* just as I turned the key in the ignition, the tune at war with the powerful throb of the engine. I never understood why my father souped-up these cars, or why he insisted that I drove the thing in the first place. I would have been quite content with a little compact car, maybe something with Bluetooth or satellite radio. Or, you know, electric windows. I didn't think that was too much to ask, but my father insisted on me driving an American classic, as he referred to the car, and since it meant no car payment, I couldn't complain too much.

"Hey, Chloe?" I greeted, cutting off the song snippet as it started again.

"Where are you?" she asked, sounding exasperated, which was something I was pretty familiar with. Chloe Tatum, my best friend – *slash* – roommate was nothing if not easily excitable, though you'd never know it by looking at her. I could already picture her lying on the sofa, dark hair fanned out around her head, emerald green eyes staring at the front door as she waited for me to come in.

"I'm leaving work," I explained, leaning my head back on the headrest and closing my eyes.

I wondered if it would be against company policy if I just slept right there in my car.

"At least tell me you're bringing dinner home."

"I can." I peered through one eye to see that the lights were slowly going out inside the two-story building in front of me. It was only seven, but since it was almost November, the days were getting shorter. That should have made me feel a little better, and it would have if I weren't still at work. I loved fall. It was my favorite time of year. Instead, I was imagining crawling into bed and sleeping away the last few days of October. "What did you have in mind?"

"Chinese."

"I'll pick it up on my way. Is Aaron home yet?" I asked, referring to our other roommate.

Aaron, my best friend since junior high school was still a student at the University of Texas, working on his master's degree in business. He and I had shared an apartment since we were sophomores in college, after each spending a year in the dorms. And when I moved farther from campus after I graduated, he had decided to come with me. Unfortunately, he wasn't home much these days, choosing to spend his evenings with his new boyfriend. Unfortunate because I didn't get to see him much, not because he had a boyfriend.

Seeing how incredibly happy Aaron was, I couldn't even find it in me to be bothered by the fact that he wasn't there for me to talk to, or to do his share of chores either. Paying a third of the rent while staying elsewhere ninety percent of the time, I figured the guy deserved a little slack. Since I'd had the pleasure of hearing all about New-Boyfriend-Mark, suffice it to say, I was actually thrilled for Aaron. He'd been looking for love for a long time, and it seemed as though he might have actually found it with Mark. At least according to him. I, personally, didn't know Mark all that well, so the jury was still out as far as I was concerned.

"Nope. He came and went an hour ago. Said he's staying with his love bunny and not to wait up."

"He said that?" I asked, my eyebrows shifting up. "He called Mark his love bunny?"

"No. I did." Chloe chuckled, obviously proud of herself.

"So dinner for two?"

"Unless you're gonna waste more time talking. Then you might as well make it three 'cause I'm starving."

"At least there won't be any traffic," I told Chloe.

"Traffic? At this time of night, you'll be lucky if there're any restaurants open," she said facetiously, following with a giggle.

I couldn't even drum up enough energy to laugh at her lame jokes, so I simply said goodbye and thumbed off the phone, dropping it onto the seat beside me.

An hour and ten freaking minutes later, I was pulling into the parking lot of my apartment complex. Since I'd had so much time to think on the way home, I'd come to one sound conclusion: there was no way I was going to survive that commute every day.

To make a bad day worse, someone had stolen my parking spot in front of my building, so I had to drive around for an extra minute until I found an empty place.

Three buildings down.

Figured.

Dreading the walk in the foot murderers that I called shoes, I was tempted to bust into the food that had been my only companion for the past half hour right there in my car. The heavenly scent of Chinese food taunted me, making my mouth water. I'd made the mistake of stopping at one of my favorite places near downtown Austin, rather than near the apartment, and I'd had to endure the overwhelming urge to eat sweet and sour pork with my fingers most of the way home.

Now, as I lugged all of my stuff toward my building, I worried that I might not be awake long enough to enjoy it at all.

When I walked in my front door a few minutes later, toting my purse on one arm, the computer bag complete with the laptop I was told to keep on me at all times, and the plastic bag holding our dinner, I was panting like I'd been floundering on the treadmill again.

Damn stairs.

"A little help would be nice," I muttered to Chloe, who was lounging on the couch, her Kindle in front of her.

She didn't budge. Not that I had really expected her to. This was Chloe. When she was focused, she made as little movement as possible, which made me hate her for the simple fact that she was so damn skinny and she never had to work out. She claimed that she kept in shape because she was on her feet all day. Did I mention Chloe was a hairstylist? One of the best, to be exact.

"Fine. I'll just eat your eggroll," I added as I passed her.

"What's *that*?" Chloe's bright green eyes homed in on the computer bag now dangling from my arm, her head turning at an odd angle so that she didn't have to get up.

"Work."

"Why're you bringing it home?" she asked, looking sincerely perplexed.

"No idea." I didn't really care to talk, I preferred to eat, so I made my way to the kitchen, letting the bag and my purse slide to the floor where I left them near my bedroom door. I kicked off my shoes, sending one flying into the wall, the other falling from my aching foot.

After pulling the containers from the bag and gathering utensils, I carried the two cartons of food and two plastic forks — screw the chopsticks, I was just too damn tired to make that happen — into the living room and joined Chloe on the couch.

"So, tell me about him," Chloe stated as she crossed her legs and dropped her Kindle onto the coffee table before reaching for the carton that contained her beef and broccoli.

"Who?" I asked, mirroring her position so I could face her. I feared that if I relaxed too much, I'd fall asleep right there.

"Conrad Trovato." Chloe annunciated his name slowly, dreamily. "He looks so handsome when I've seen him on TV."

I cocked an eyebrow. "Seriously? He's like fifty," I told her, laughing around a mouthful of food.

"That just means he's distinguished," Chloe countered, forking rice into her mouth.

"It also means he's married."

"True. For like the third time if I remember correctly." Chloe kept eating, her full attention on the food in front of her as she continued talking, oblivious to the fact that her mouth was full. "Does he have any kids?"

When she peered up at me, I shrugged.

"You don't *know*? What kind of assistant are you?" Chloe huffed.

"He's got a daughter, I think." I paused, chewing thoroughly, purposely making her wait. "He's got her picture in his office."

"You sure that's his daughter and not his wife?" Chloe asked. "Or his mistress?"

God, I hoped not. The girl was young and he was… not.

"How old is she?" Chloe inquired before I could even answer.

"She's in college. Aside from that, I didn't bombard him with personal questions on my first day."

"I would have." I totally believed her. "Seriously, Payton. This is Conrad Trovato. He's the mastermind behind those engines that make your girl parts sing."

My eyes nearly bugged out of my head. "Sorry, my girl parts don't sing for engines." Hell, these days, my girl parts didn't sing for anyone.

"Oh, come on. How freaking hot is it when one of those things starts up? I still don't know how you can drive your Mustang and not have an orgasm every damn day. Did you ask him how they make them do that?"

I laughed, nearly choking on my sweet and sour pork. Chloe's mouth did not have a filter; that was for sure. "No, I didn't."

"Well, you should," Chloe said seriously.

No, I shouldn't. I should just do my job and maybe, just maybe, I'd be able to save up a little money to move to a city where I could find a job I actually enjoyed. I didn't share that little tidbit of internal monologue with Chloe.

"Wait!" Chloe exclaimed, snatching up the fortune cookies sitting on the couch between us. She tossed one my way. "Open it," Chloe demanded as she cracked open her cookie and smiled.

Oh, the dreaded fortune cookie. This had become a ritual for us anytime we picked up Chinese to go, which was about once a week these days. The rule was that we had to open the cookie before we ever finished our meal. If there was a particular protocol around reading those things, I was pretty sure we'd mucked that up a long time ago.

Placing the container on my leg, I followed suit, tearing the plastic wrapper and then breaking the cookie. I stared at the message, blinking several times as I did.

"What does yours say?" Chloe asked inquisitively.

Glancing up, I met her eyes. "Uh…" My attention slid back to the paper. "It says 'Get ready for something to shake up your life.'"

Chloe sighed heavily. "Lucky you. Mine says 'You'll take a trip to Asia.' I mean, come on. That's not a fortune. Asia. Right. Like I'll ever be that lucky."

I stared at the paper in my hand, wondering for once if it might come true. I needed something to come along and give my life a little shake.

Not that I wanted to think about that now. Right now, I just wanted to finish my food and pray that my feet would carry me the short distance to my bedroom.

After all, I still had to get up and do it all again tomorrow.

Chapter Three

Payton

I knew I was asleep. I had to be. Even knowing that, I was having a hard time deciphering the dream from reality. There was no way this could be real. Could it?

I didn't want to wake up. I didn't want to lose this moment.

This guy, whoever he was, he mesmerized me, drew me in. I couldn't pull my eyes away, couldn't break the spell he had on me. Something in the way he walked, talked, moved.

Breathed.

So familiar, yet not.

I felt like I knew him, like I'd met him before, but for the life of me I don't remember any such encounter. Had we met? Was this my mind conjuring up the image of something from my past? Or was this some sort of vision from the future?

Either way, I didn't want to open my eyes. Didn't want to face reality if he wasn't in it. I wanted to get closer, to look into his eyes, to know what he was thinking.

I was unabashedly staring, unable to look away.

Whoever he was, there was something about him...

Something that unhinged me.

My eyes flew opened and I stared at the ceiling. My heart was racing, my skin hot to the touch. The blankets were twisted around my feet, trapping me. I glanced around my bedroom. The dim glow from my computer's screen saver allowed me to see.

There was my desk, my dresser, the few pictures I had hanging on the wall.

And just as I feared, I was alone.

There was no one there. No handsome stranger.

Blinking a few times, I willed the dream to come back. I knew that no matter how hard I tried, I wouldn't be able to close my eyes and bring him back, but I wanted to. Oh, how I wanted to.

Rolling over onto my side, I tugged the blankets from between my feet, pulling them over me. I squeezed my eyes shut again, hoping he would come back.

I had no idea who he was; I just wanted him back.

Chapter Four

Payton

(Just shy of) two weeks later
Thursday

"Payton!"

"Damn it," I grumbled under my breath, reaching for a napkin from the stash on my desk.

You'd think that after two weeks of this, I'd be used to Mr. Trovato shouting at me from his office.

Nope. Still not used to it.

He once again startled me, and now I had coffee dripping from my hand and down the front of my favorite off-white V-neck sweater. I knew I should have started drinking my coffee with a straw. Then maybe I wouldn't keep having these mishaps.

"Another one bites the dust," I mumbled as I got to my feet, wiping my hand and blotting the coffee on my chest, knowing that it wasn't going to do any good. The good news, if there was any, was that this sweater didn't have to be dry cleaned.

You'd think I would learn to stop wearing light colored clothing.

One of the perks of the job I found out was that I didn't have to dress up unless Mr. Trovato was expecting a client, or a high-level employee, to show up. Today was one of those days when I was supposed to be ready to greet the sales director, which was why I was wearing one of my favorite skirts and a sweater I'd fallen in love with and picked up on sale last week after I received my first paycheck.

I hadn't wanted to go shopping, but I hadn't had much of a choice. Unfortunately, I'd learned about the casual dress code from Maude, the snarky old receptionist on the main floor, *after* she and Ron, the security guard, spent several days making bets on whether or not I would ask about it. Had Maude not felt guilty for taking Ron's money, she probably would've let me go on looking like a wannabe executive. As it turned out, Ron had no intention of telling me since he found my thrift store wardrobe — his words — rather amusing. Hence, the reason for my shopping trip.

I grabbed my notepad and started toward Mr. Trovato's office, swiping at the brown spot in the center of my chest. Two weeks of this and I was ready to show him how to use the phone's intercom because his yelling was starting to be a problem for my wardrobe.

Not that I would *ever* tell him that.

Holding my pen and paper close to my chest in order to hide the newly forming stain, I approached his office.

"Yes, sir?" I asked as I stood in his open doorway.

Conrad, as always, looked well-put together in his dark suit, crisp white shirt and bright red tie. His face was clean shaven, his reading glasses perched on his long, thin nose, and on his head, not a single gray hair out of place. By noon, I knew he would've lost the jacket, the tie would be dangling from the back of his chair, and his sleeves would've been rolled up to his elbows, so I often wondered why he even bothered with the whole get up each day.

He had actually freaked me out last Friday when he came in wearing jeans and a black polo. Even in his fifties, the guy could rock a pair of distressed jeans. I just hadn't expected it.

"I need you to run to my house," he told me, reaching for the landline phone on his desk.

Umm… what?

"Sir?" I knew, should he actually turn and look at me, that Conrad would see my bewilderment written right across my face. And it wouldn't be the first time either. He was randomly asking me to do odd things, such as go out to his car and get his briefcase, or look up one of his old buddies from college, or once he even had me go down to the mechanic garage and get a wrench.

No, I didn't ask.

But his house?

"I left my cell phone at home and my wife can't bring it to me." Conrad continued as he placed the receiver to his ear. "I need it before my afternoon meeting."

Well, that explained why Mrs. Trovato had called the main number three times that morning and it was only ten.

"Umm…" I wasn't quite sure what to say. Where did he live? Was I just supposed to ask him?

"Just ask, Payton." Mr. Trovato was apparently reading my mind. He was also smiling, which I took as a good sign. I was pretty sure I amused him to no end, but luckily he'd been patient with me so far.

"I don't have your address," I blurted.

"That wasn't a question," he informed me.

No, it wasn't. I took a deep breath and met his intimidating stare from across the room. "I feel like I should know this."

"Have you had a reason to go to my house?"

"No, sir."

"Then you probably shouldn't know my address. My daughter Aaliyah is home. She'll be there for the next half hour, but then she has class. So you better get going."

I didn't bother asking him why Aaliyah couldn't bring the phone because that really wouldn't have gone over well. I was his assistant and, as I had recently learned, if he yelled, I was supposed to jump.

I was getting good at that.

"Yes, sir," I said by rote, turning around to walk out. Only when I was a few feet away did I realize that I never got his address.

"I'll email it to you, Payton," Mr. Trovato called from behind me, his tone full of amusement.

Swallowing hard, I nodded although I knew he couldn't see me.

As I walked back to my desk, I remembered Jasmine's parting words: *It'll get easier as time goes by.*

I was starting to wonder just how much time it was going to take.

Chapter Five

Payton

Twenty-seven minutes later, I was waiting at the gates to a mansion. Mr. Trovato's mansion to be exact. I had made good time, but only because I had nixed the idea of stopping for coffee on my way over. It had been a tough decision, but I had decided I would do my best not to screw this up too much. After all, Mr. Trovato was expecting me back soon.

I had entered Conrad's address in the navigation app on my cell phone and found that he didn't live too far from the office. I didn't know the area at all, but my trusty phone had gotten me here. It took twenty minutes to get to the sprawling neighborhood, and another seven for me to drive slowly down the streets, up one hill, down another. As I drove, I admired the elaborate, multi-million dollar houses with their perfectly manicured lawns all while trying to locate the two-story white house — Conrad's exact description — that belonged to my boss.

I had finally resorted to looking at the numbers on the large stone pillars in front of each house until finally I found it. Good thing too because there wasn't a house in sight.

From where I sat in my car, waiting for the security guard to approach, I couldn't see past the narrow road lined with trees in front of me, but the ostentatious wrought iron fence that surrounded the property told me enough.

After manually rolling down the window, — have I mentioned how much I hate that — I peered up at the young man with a military style haircut, and forced a smile.

"Can I help you?" the intimidating guard asked, his tone level, his eyes narrowed.

"My name's Payton Fowler. I work for Mr. Trovato. He sent me here to pick up his cell phone."

"License."

Arguing didn't seem appropriate, nor did asking him to say please, so I dug in my purse for my wallet, noticing in my peripheral vision that the guard had put his hand on his gun. What did he think I was going to do? Assault him with a little plastic card so I could raid the property and steal Mr. Trovato's cell phone?

I tossed him a smile over my shoulder as I pulled my license from my wallet before handing it to him.

"Just a minute."

I nodded.

As I waited for the security guard to finish scrutinizing my driver's license, I glanced around the grounds that I could see. Aside from the ornate iron work of the fence, I could see trees. Lots and lots of them. A long row of them flanked the narrow drive that led into the estate. I didn't know much about trees, but they looked a lot like the ones that were in my parents' yard. Pecan maybe. Not that it really mattered, but I didn't have anything else to do except to study the landscape.

On the side of the gate that I was on, there was a small guard station with two windows. It had been painted white, but the door was red, which I found odd. There was a fancy looking golf cart parked beside it. I assumed that was security's way of checking the perimeter. That, or the house was miles away and they needed it to get back and forth.

I glanced at the clock on my phone. Yep, my thirty minutes was up. If this guy didn't hurry, I was going to miss Aaliyah.

"You're good to go," the security guard said when he finally returned, his severe expression hadn't changed. He still looked like someone had shoved his night stick up his butt and left it there.

"Thank you," I replied sweetly, reaching for my license.

When the gate opened, I put my foot on the gas, embarrassed by the way that the engine roared, all throaty and loud. The guard didn't seem to mind. If anything, he was eyeing the car with appreciation.

I got that a lot. Especially from men. They seemed to admire the car. The most awkward moments were when they wanted to talk about it. I think it frustrated them when they found out I actually knew a little bit about what was under the hood — 302 cubic inches of Ford Racing V8 with a Vortech supercharger that turned 444 Dyno-proven horsepower into 423 pounds of stump-pulling torque. Yep, it was safe to say that I'd learned a little from my father when it came to cars.

The car certainly garnered more head turns than I did though. But since I'd spent four years working diligently to get my degree, it wasn't like I'd had any time to date anyway.

Or at least that's what I told myself.

Truth was, I don't think it had much to do with my busy schedule. It was more due to the fact that I was just a little too plain. I wasn't tall or supermodel thin, my legs weren't long, and I had an average face. My nose was a little too pointy in my opinion, and my cheekbones a little too prominent. The only interesting thing about me was the color of my eyes, or so I'd been told. Cat eyes, I had heard the color referred to as. Kind of hazel, though more green than brown, but they were constantly changing and sometimes appeared almost yellow.

My hair was naturally a mousy brown and would still be if it weren't for the magic hands — and a steep discount — of my hair stylist, Chloe. The girl was certainly my savior when it came to looking good.

After following the winding road through the trees, I came upon the two-story white house Conrad had mentioned.

Right.

Like *that* could be considered a house.

I actually hit the brakes as soon as it came into view because I was so taken aback, I forgot where the gas pedal was. And the clutch, which was why the car died. I had to restart the engine before pulling forward.

In the last week, I'd spent a considerable amount of time researching Conrad Trovato. Mostly when I had nothing else to do. I figured it couldn't hurt to know everything there was to know about the guy.

From what I gathered, he'd made his first million roughly twenty years ago. It wasn't until the last decade or so years that he'd hit the Forbe's World's Billionaires list though. Not that a few hundred million was anything to tip your nose at, but Trovato, Inc. had been put on the map when some car manufacturer wanted to use one of their super-charged performance engines for one of their new lines of sports cars, tying the names together — similar to what Carroll Shelby did with Ford back in the 60s. On top of that, the car company had been featured in movies, which had brought a significant amount of exposure to Trovato, Inc.

Based on what I was seeing in front of me, Mr. Trovato and his family weren't hurting.

I'm not sure what I had expected, but it wasn't to be met at the gate by a security guard, or to find two more waving me by when I reached the circular drive in front of the white monstrosity that obviously acted as the Trovato's residence.

It looked like the White House. And not just because it was white either.

It was… big.

Oddly, that was the only word that came to mind. As I climbed out of the car, I was too busy taking everything in from the freshly clipped lawn, to the extravagant flowerbeds and towering trees to think about the house. There was even one of those fancy water fountains in the center of the circular drive — just like in the movies.

Someone cleared their throat.

I spun around to see a short, older man standing on the front steps wearing a…

Hmmm.

I was beginning to think maybe I was in a movie.

He looked like he was wearing a butler's uniform. Since I'd only ever seen a butler on the big screen, I'm not even sure if that was an accurate description, but I nodded my head at him anyway. Glancing down into my car, I decided to leave my purse but snatched my cell phone just in case.

When I stood back up, the man/butler was gone, but coming toward me was another guy. This one wasn't sporting a nifty suit and was much, much younger. The sun was shining brightly overhead, making it difficult for me to see him clearly, but the first word that came to mind was… wow.

I pulled my sunglasses off and started walking toward him, trying not to gawk. He was lean and tall, powerfully built with a broad chest and wide shoulders. My breath hitched in my throat as the distance between us slowly disappeared. There was something strangely familiar about him. Like I'd met him before.

When I was close enough to take in his appearance altogether, I noticed he was wearing a white tank top that clung to the hard lines of his chiseled torso and had grease smudged across the front. His arms, from his shoulders to his elbows, were tan, muscular and covered in tattoos. Most of the designs were tribal art as well as some words that I couldn't make out. My gaze continued south, noticing he had on tattered jeans that hung low on his narrow hips, and brown, lace-up work boots.

He was wiping his hands on a thin, red towel as he sauntered toward me.

Yes, the guy sauntered. I mean he had some serious swagger, but it was sexy. Too sexy.

I cleared my throat, trying to rein in my body's strange reaction to him.

Did I know him?

The gap between us slowly diminished and, as I got closer, I tried to make out his face, but the sun was shining from behind him, outlining his body, but making it impossible to make out his facial features.

Maybe he was a mechanic or something. Did rich people have mechanics?

"Can I help you?"

The dark, rough sound of his voice had my gaze traveling north, my eyes darting up to meet his.

I stopped.

Right there, just a few feet away, I just stopped moving, my entire body going on alert.

There was an eerie sense of déjà vu, like I'd met him before.

What happened next could only be described as cataclysmic.

My hand came up to my mouth as I sucked in a breath. He was…

Holy crap.

He was the guy from my dream. The dream I'd had for the last couple of weeks. He was the guy I couldn't look away from, the one I would try to call back just before I would awaken abruptly. That was him. At least I thought it was.

There were still several feet between us, but as I looked up at his face, studying his ruggedly handsome features, I knew it was him.

Every man I'd ever met escaped my mind and the only thing I could think about was this incredibly good-looking guy standing there, his head tilted sideways as though he was studying me. The expression on his face could only be described as confused, almost like he was having a weird moment of déjà vu, too. Similar to the way I was feeling.

I could tell he was much taller than I was. Over six-feet. He looked young. Mid-twenties if I had to guess. Aside from his well-built body, his hair was short and brown, but it wasn't dark and it wasn't light. Somewhere neatly in between. There were blond streaks in the longer strands on top, as though he spent a lot of time outside and the sun had highlighted various pieces. His jaw was scruffy, as was his chin. I don't think it was meant to be a beard. More like he'd forgotten to shave that morning.

But his eyes…

Oh, heaven help me. The guy had eyes that paralyzed me in place. They were a vibrant, liquid gold. But it wasn't necessarily the color that had me nearly tripping over my own two feet. There was something in those eyes that spoke of sex. And danger. The sexy kind of danger that girls like me ran away from.

I wasn't running, but based on the way my heart rate accelerated, I'm not sure my respiratory system realized that I was still standing in place.

The guy cleared his throat, repeating his question.

"I'm…"

Who the hell am I?

At first, I couldn't break the penetrating stare and when I finally did, I allowed my gaze to rake over his face, admiring the hard angles, the ruggedly handsome features. I would even have to admit that the silver barbell piercing in his left eyebrow was sexy. But I found myself transfixed on his mouth and when his lips parted ever so slightly, I saw that he had a silver ring on his lower lip, right in the center, the metal glinting in the sun.

"Help me out here, Angel. I'm not sure who you're here to see."

Did he just call me angel?

Remembering why I was there, I took the remaining steps to close the gap between us and I held out my hand to him. "I'm Payton Fowler. I came to see Aaliyah."

The guy glanced down at my hand and then back to my face. He left me hanging, so I tried to pretend I wasn't humiliated, switching my cell phone to that hand and clutching it tightly.

"Ahh, one of Aaliyah's little friends. Sorry, you just missed her." Humor danced in his honey-gold eyes as he looked above my head.

I didn't bother to correct his assumption that Aaliyah and I were friends because the sound of an engine caught my attention. I glanced over my shoulder in time to see a Mercedes speeding down the narrow drive. I could only assume that was Aaliyah.

"Well, crap." I realized I spoke my thoughts aloud. Meeting the guy's gaze once more, I followed with, "Do you work here?"

The smile that tipped his full lips had my knees going weak momentarily. I got a glimpse of bright white teeth along with the glint from his lip ring.

"You could say that," he answered.

"And you are?" I asked, needing to snap out of it and get on with the reason I was there. I had a job to do, and Mr. Trovato would be expecting me back in the office before he left for his afternoon meeting with one of the senior vice presidents.

"Name's Sebastian. Don't worry, Angel, I'm sure she'll be back after class."

Crap. Crap. Crap.

That wasn't going to help me now. It wasn't like I could sit around and wait for her to get back just to ask if she had her father's phone.

"Would you know if…," I glanced over at the front door, "if anyone else is home? I'm supposed to pick up Mr. Trovato's cell phone. He told me Aaliyah would be here to give it to me."

"Nope. No one else here," he said confidently as he slung the red rag over his shoulder and thrust his hands into his pockets, the muscles in his thick arms bulging, the black designs that twisted around his arms flexing and moving.

He was breathtaking.

But that wasn't why I was there.

I cocked an eyebrow as I contemplated my next move. I had seen the butler/man standing on the front porch, so I was pretty sure *someone* was home. When Sebastian didn't seem to want to change his answer, I knew I'd hit a brick wall.

Damn. Damn. Damn.

This day wasn't getting any better; that was for damn sure.

When I squinted up at Sebastian one last time, I found his gaze had drifted down to my chest. Feeling incredibly exposed, I immediately covered my breasts by crossing my arms. "Hello-o-o." I made sure he heard my annoyance. "My eyes are up here."

"Sorry," he responded with a smirk, looking not at all sorry. "You've got a stain on your sweater."

As though I didn't know the stain was there, I glanced down at my chest, realizing that by crossing my arms, I'd thrust my boobs up, increasing the amount of cleavage peeking out from the very modest V-neck of my sweater.

"Coffee," I said inanely.

Sebastian met my gaze and grinned before glancing over his shoulder. "I guess I should get back to work."

I nodded, not sure what else I could do. If this guy insisted that no one was home, I couldn't just walk right in even if I suspected otherwise. And I seriously doubted the Trovato's wanted their mechanic traipsing through their house looking for Conrad's cell phone.

Without so much as a goodbye, Sebastian turned and walked away.

That's when I realized that the earth-shattering impact of seeing him for the first time was suddenly overshadowed by the vision of him walking away. Although his jeans were loose, I could still see the shape of his perfect ass behind the soft denim.

On hearing his sexy, gruff chuckle, I immediately looked up and that's when I realized he'd caught me ogling his ass.

At least now I didn't have to worry about Mr. Trovato firing me.

It wasn't going to matter since I was surely going to die of mortification anyway.

Chapter Six

Sebastian

Holy shit.

That was her.

That was the girl from my dream.

As I walked back to the garage, I did my best not to turn around and watch her drive away.

I had to give myself a little credit. I think I handled myself pretty damn well considering I'd been shocked as soon as I saw her. She was the girl I had been dreaming about for the last few nights.

Stepping into the shadows of the garage, memories of my dream came back with a vengeance, and I stopped moving as the vision replayed inside my head.

I knew I was asleep. I had to be. Even knowing that, I was having a hard time deciphering the dream from reality. There was no way this could be real. Could it?

I didn't want to wake up. I didn't want to lose this moment.

She, whoever she was, she mesmerized me, drew me in. I couldn't pull my eyes away, couldn't break the spell she had on me. Something in the way she walked, talked, moved.

Breathed.

So familiar, yet not.

I felt like I knew her, like I'd met her before, but for the life of me I don't remember any such encounter. Had we met? Was this my mind conjuring up the image of something from my past? Or was this some sort of vision from the future?

Either way, I didn't want to open my eyes. Didn't want to face reality if she wasn't in it. I wanted to get closer, to look into her eyes, to know what she was thinking.

I was unabashedly staring, unable to look away.

Whoever she was, there was something about her…

Something that unhinged me.

Unfortunately, every time the dream got that far, my eyes would come open, the dream drifting off into nothingness. No matter how hard I tried to call it back, it never worked. Just that morning, I'd lay motionless in my bed, my chest heaving, my heart pounding while the first rays of the early morning sun peeked in my bedroom window. After getting my breathing under control, I had glanced at my alarm clock. Groaning, I then rolled over, refusing to get up at six.

But I was awake now. Completely. Payton Fowler, she was the girl from my dream. And she'd been standing right there in the driveway, looking just as she had in my dream.

Well, save for the outfit. She hadn't been wearing that prissy skirt when I'd dreamed about her. No, she'd had on jeans and a T-shirt, her cute little feet were bare. Her long, dark hair had been pulled back in a ponytail, not hanging loosely over her shoulders. But her smile, the smoothness of her alabaster skin, her pert little nose, those full lips and the way her hazel eyes had lit up when she looked at me… It had all been the same. Every last detail.

"Do I work here, she asked?" I was grumbling to myself as I made my way back to the truck where the stupid ass engine was waiting for me. "Yep, Angel, I work here all right," I mused aloud.

From the moment I laid eyes on her, I'd nearly tripped over my own two feet. It had been surreal, and for a brief moment, I'd wondered if I were asleep again.

I pinched myself, the pain ricocheting up my arm.

Nope, not dreaming. She was real.

And now I was smiling. Even as I resumed my place in the garage where I spent most of my time, — in my world, eight bays, air conditioning and a kickass sound system equaled a garage — the smirk was still plastered on my face.

I thought maybe the muscles were stuck or something. I didn't spend much time smiling these days and certainly not today.

Until I'd heard the guttural purr of the Mustang pulling up, I'd spent the better part of the last three hours fiddling with the damn engine on my cherry red, '63 Chevy truck, yet it was still idling too fucking high. Since the engine was a prototype that I was working on in my spare time, I was used to the minor quirks from the damn thing, but for the life of me, I couldn't get the bugs out of this one.

"Stupid ass engine," I groaned loudly.

After that interruption, I doubted I'd be able to get my mind back in gear. That woman — Payton — had single-handedly knocked me for a loop there for a second. From the moment I saw her walking toward me in those killer fucking heels, I'd had a damn hard time keeping my boner at bay.

I felt like I'd just stepped into a bad porno — the kind where the hot, young executive woman meets the mechanic and things get hot fast.

Yeah, that hadn't happened.

I had reined in my instant primitive reaction to her, but my lust had been quickly replaced with confusion.

At first, I thought I'd met her before, but when I heard the lyrical sound of her voice, I realized there was no way. I would have remembered her. But there had been something niggling in my head. I may not have met her, but I'd certainly seen her before. That was when I remembered the dream.

That chick was fucking hot, even if that outfit didn't do a damn thing for her. The way her glossy brown hair sparkled in the sunlight... It was the first thing I noticed, but certainly not the last.

"Did I work here?" I repeated, grinning.

Thrusting my hands into my hair, I stared at the engine that was hell bent on dissolving my patience.

And still I was smiling.

Conrad's new assistant, huh? Interesting.

My amusement still didn't die off even as I accepted the fact that, by working for Conrad, Ms. Fowler was technically off limits to me.

My grin widened.

Right. Like that had ever stopped me before.

It wasn't until she mentioned her name that I realized who she was, but that hadn't quelled the notion that I'd seen her before. For the last two weeks, Conrad had been going on and on about the new assistant he had, but it wasn't like I'd been introduced to her yet. Needless to say, Conrad didn't make a habit of introducing me to the women in his office. I doubted that was going to change anytime soon either.

While I'd stood there studying her, I tried to convince myself that the only reason she sounded familiar was the fact that Conrad had been talking about her for the last couple of weeks. I think he was still trying to convince himself that she would work out, eventually, but he had plenty of concerns regarding her ability to do the job.

She was an assistant for chrissakes. How fucking hard could that be?

Not that I'd asked him. I didn't really give a fuck, truth be told.

The only time I'd uttered a word had been when he admitted that he missed his old assistant, Jasmine. I, personally, was grateful that the snooty bitch was gone, and I'd told him as much. If anyone could make me feel like a two-bit reject, it had been Jasmine.

Then again, that's what happened when you were in the shadows, pretending you were nothing more than an employee who was paid extra to make house calls. Right. Like I'd willingly work for Conrad if there wasn't something in it for me.

Retrieving the grease rag from my shoulder, I carried it over to the Mercedes-Benz SLR McLaren that I'd been tinkering with the last few days. Some hot shot millionaire that Conrad knew was willing to pay an absurd amount of money to have the damn thing supercharged. As if half a mil wasn't enough to drop on a car already, now he was willing to pay *my* price to make the damn thing go faster — in a way only I knew how.

Like the asshole could handle the speed in the first place.

While I grabbed my tools, I let my mind drift back to my brief encounter with Payton a few minutes before.

Yeah, I know. I should have probably told her who I was, but she seemed to have drawn her own conclusion already. I didn't want to disappoint her.

The mechanic.

That actually made me laugh.

Technically, it was true. But I wasn't the *family's* mechanic. I was the brains behind the stupid Trovato fortune, although Conrad would never willingly admit as much. He took full credit and I pretended that I wasn't bothered by it. Hell, he was the one responsible for convincing the media that I was nothing more than a lowly employee of Trovato, Inc., but I certainly hadn't tried to correct him.

Little did they know.

It would probably blow their fucking minds to know that if it weren't for me, Trovato, Inc. would still be moving along at a snail's pace, trying to come up with a performance engine that all the damn car manufacturers were looking for these days. Then again, there were even bigger secrets that they'd latch onto if they had the chance.

But, I wasn't looking for glory or acknowledgement.

In fact, I preferred to spend my days entangled in an engine or screwing around on the computer away from the cogs of the company. Even if I wanted to, I would never fit in there. Hell, I barely fit in here.

So, Conrad and I had come to an agreement, he would leave me the hell alone, and I would, in turn, make him more money.

As for me, I wasn't hurting.

At twenty-five, I had enough that my grandkids would never have to work. But that was only one of my secrets. You see, I happen to be the heir to the Trovato fortune... Conrad Trovato's illegitimate son. So, yeah, lowly mechanic I wasn't.

"You're a dumbass, Trovato."

Yep, I'd gotten used to talking to myself. Today was no exception.

I could've let Payton in the house because I happened to live here, too. Although I didn't live in the main house. That wouldn't have been pleasant for anyone involved, just ask my stepmother — the woman who despised me probably more than Conrad did — or my half-sister Aaliyah.

No, I chose to live on my father's estate, in the guest house, of course. The guest house was four-thousand square feet, mind you, so I certainly wasn't slumming it. I wasn't there because the prospect of family made me leery to leave either. No, I was there for convenience. Pure and simple.

The chirp of my cell phone across the room had me ducking out from beneath the hood and wiping my hands again. Seeing that it was my father, I was tempted to ignore it. I knew without answering just what he had to say.

"Yo," I greeted after putting the phone on speaker.

My father hated that.

"Where are you?" he asked, the frustration in his tone echoing through the cavernous space.

"Garage. Why?"

"Where's Aaliyah?"

"School." Not that I was her keeper or anything.

"Why the hell did you tell Payton that no one was home?"

"I didn't know her from Eve," I lied. "What was I supposed to do? Let her in to rummage through the house?"

In case I hadn't mentioned it, I lived to torment my father. We had a love/hate relationship that we'd perfected over the last few years — ever since I was introduced to him.

You see, I'm Conrad Trovato's dirty little secret. Or my mother was anyway.

Needless to say, we didn't particularly like each other, although he'd insisted on taking me in when my mother died. I'd been fourteen at the time, and since I didn't have any other family willing to take in a wild kid with a growing juvenile record, I hadn't had much of a choice.

I was still wild, more so now. The only difference was that I didn't get caught anymore.

Conrad didn't appreciate my wild living, and I didn't appreciate how he had treated my mother. Or the way he talked down to me. We'd come to an impasse before I was twenty-one and the years hadn't improved our relationship one fucking bit.

"I need my phone," he groused.

"Come and get it," I snapped.

"Sebastian," Conrad chastised, drawing my name out in way too many syllables.

I didn't say anything.

"You need to grow up, Sebastian," he finally added.

And you need to go to hell, I thought to myself.

"Was there something else?" I asked, pretending my head wasn't about to explode.

"Actually, there is," he stated.

Damn.

I bit my tongue, knowing he would eventually say something.

"We're having a party tomorrow night."

"Great. Have fun."

Unfortunately, Conrad and his wife Lauren had a penchant for throwing parties all the damned time. They claimed they were for charity, but I knew better. My stepmother loved the limelight. She loved to show off her riches and inviting other affluent assholes to their home was the easiest way for her to do that.

"We're announcing the new concept car."

Fucking shit.

"I want you to be there."

"Not a chance in hell," I told him firmly. Rather than argue because I know the next phase, I simply added, "Look, I gotta work." With that, I hung up on him.

I'd hear all about it the next time I saw him, I was sure. The old man lived to bust my balls, which didn't make me want to do him any favors.

Chapter Seven

Payton

"Party?" I stared back at Mr. Trovato, praying my mouth wasn't hanging open while I tried to comprehend what he'd just asked me.

I was pretty sure my jaw was on the floor.

I'd been back in the office for all of an hour, eating my turkey sandwich at my desk while Mr. Trovato left to attend his lunch meeting. He'd been gone less time than I figured he would be and when he returned, I had been filing some paperwork that had been signed last week. I had greeted him as soon as he reached the top of the stairs, and on his way to his office he had mumbled something about a party.

Yes, a party.

Maybe I was hearing things because it sure sounded like Conrad had invited me to a party at his house.

He stopped in the doorway, his hand on the frame as he turned back toward me. "Tomorrow night. Seven o'clock. Black tie. My house. I'll make sure you're added to the guest list," Mr. Trovato clarified.

Yep, it was official. I wasn't hearing things.

I nodded, purely because I had no idea what to say.

As much as I liked my job, despite the bizarre encounter I'd had with Mr. Trovato's mechanic, or the peculiar expression I'd been met with when I explained to Conrad before he left for lunch — for the second time — what had happened, I wasn't all that interested in going to a party.

"Mr. Trovato?" I greeted when Conrad answered his office phone *after Maude so kindly transferred me to him.*

"Yes, Payton?"

It sure sounded like Mr. Trovato had been expecting me to call, but I pretended not to notice. "I wasn't able to get your cell phone, sir. Aaliyah had already left for school and your mechanic said that no one was home."

"My mechanic?"

"Yes, sir."

"Umm… Okay. Just come back to the office, Payton."

"Yes, sir."

I thought I'd heard a hitch in my boss's voice when I called to inform him I wasn't able to get his phone as I was driving back to the office. But the look on his face when I told him in person was… priceless.

In fact, he probably looked a lot like I did right at that moment.

What was I going to do at a party at his house? Certainly he wasn't expecting me to assist him. Was he?

Oh, crap. Now I was even more worried.

Between that and trying to figure out what to wear…

It was bad enough that I didn't have anything to wear to work. Now I had to figure out what to wear to a party. Black tie? That meant I had to wear something fancy, right?

Shit.

"Will you be able to make it, Payton?" Conrad asked, pulling me from my wayward thoughts.

"Yes, sir." The words had come out before I thought better of it.

Crap.

"Great. I'll let my wife know to add you. I'll be back in two hours," Mr. Trovato stated as he headed toward the stairs.

Again, I nodded.

Lowering myself into my chair, I dropped my head into my hands and tried to put the errant thoughts running through my mind into some sort of order.

Sexy mechanic. Didn't need to think about.

What to wear to a party. Top priority.

Who would go with me? Good question.

Sexy mechanic.

Ugghhh!

It wasn't working.

Despite the fact that I had more important things to focus on, I was still attempting to replay the conversation I'd had with Sebastian and how it was possible that I'd had a dream about a guy I'd never met. It still didn't make sense. On top of that, I was trying to figure out why I couldn't stop thinking about him *period*. He had called me angel. Angel. Seriously. If that wasn't some sort of patronizing assholishness (yes, I just made that word up), I don't know what was.

Not that I had time to think about Sebastian, or our strange encounter, or whether or not he was really the mechanic. After my conversation with Conrad, I wasn't so sure that was the case. But either way, Conrad didn't seem at all concerned, so I wasn't sure why I was.

Dress.

I had to find a dress.

Yanking my cell phone out of my desk drawer, I quickly dialed Chloe's number. If anyone could help me, she could.

"I've got a problem," I said in a rush as soon as she answered.

"You've got many, but now probably isn't the time for me to point those out. What's up?"

"Thanks. I feel so much better," I retorted, gripping the phone hard enough to nearly crack the plastic. "I need a dress."

"For?"

"And a date," I continued, ignoring Chloe's question. "I need a dress and a date. Shit. Not necessarily in that order."

"Hold up, woman." Chloe laughed. "I'm sure I've got a dress you can borrow."

"Have you seen me?" I asked her, incredulity dripping from every word. "You're like three sizes smaller than I am."

"Whatever. When do you need it by?"

"Tomorrow."

"Seriously? You couldn't give me a little more notice?" she asked, teasing me as always.

"I just found out. Conrad invited me to a party. At his house."

"Girl, should I be worried that he invited you to his house?"

"Shut up." I immediately wondered what she was going to say when she found out I'd already gone to his house. "Can you help me or not?"

"With the dress, yes. If you're asking me to be your date, well, I'm afraid to tell you that you're just not my type."

I laughed, releasing the breath I'd been holding.

"What time will you be home?" Chloe asked. "And yes, I've got something that'll work, you just have to trust me."

"I won't leave here until six or so."

"Well, grab dinner on your way home and I'll work my magic."

"What do I do about a date?" I asked. It was one thing to find a dress, something else entirely to conjure up a date on such short notice.

"What about Aaron?"

Hmm… That wasn't a bad idea actually. He was my best friend, and I hadn't asked him for any favors lately. "I'll call him."

"Text me and tell me what he says. I'll see you at home tonight."

I hung up without saying goodbye, my stomach suddenly churning with nerves. I wasn't worried that Aaron would tell me no if I asked him to accompany me. The worry came from the fact that he was so busy lately and I didn't know what his plans were for tomorrow night.

But, I wasn't going to know until I tried.

Pulling up the contact list on my phone, I scrolled until I found Aaron's number and hit *dial*.

"What's up, Buttercup?" Aaron greeted on the second ring, a smile in his always cheerful voice.

"I need a date," I blurted. I followed my little outburst with a nervous giggle. I could feel my face heat. Thank goodness he wasn't there to see me. He'd laugh.

"What? Like to prom?" he asked deadpan, and just like that all of my tension drained.

Resting my forehead on my palm, my elbow on my desk, I held the phone to my ear and took a deep breath.

"Yes, to prom," I said sweetly. "I need a date to prom."

"Awesome. Count me in. When and where?"

"I'm being serious, Aaron."

"I know, doll. If you weren't serious, you wouldn't've called me."

"That's not true and you know it," I answered defensively.

Aaron responded with a snort.

He was truly my best friend. He understood me in ways even Chloe couldn't. We had a long history together and it started back when I met him in seventh grade. He was a new kid at my school. A *hot* new kid at my school. I remember noticing him for the first time. He'd been standing outside the principal's office and I had been going there for who knows what. As I passed, he tossed me a smirk and a muttered hello. Needless to say, Aaron was the first boy I ever *noticed*. Tall and gorgeous, I'd been in love at the first hello.

Me and the rest of the seventh-grade female population.

It wasn't until high school when Aaron came out of the closet that I realized we'd been destined to be friends. He admitted that he'd known that all along, but he hadn't wanted to hurt my feelings. Being rejected by a guy was mortifying, especially in high school, and Aaron had made sure never to do that to me. So, when he told me he was gay, I can't say that I was shocked. Relieved, maybe. Although I had reprimanded him for not telling me sooner. I had spent the better part of junior high thinking there was something wrong with me.

And from that moment on, my attraction to him fizzled and turned into a love that I'd never known for another person who was not my mother or father. Aaron was my best friend, I loved him like a brother and I would do anything for him. I considered myself lucky, because I knew he'd do the same for me.

"What shall I wear?" he asked.

"A tux."

"Seriously, Payton? You can't just invite me to a cool party, can you? Always makin' me dress up and shit."

"I know. I'm sorry." The last time we'd gone out had been our senior prom, so he wasn't joking.

"No worries. It's about time I donned a tux again. Mark won't know what hit him when he sees me."

There was so much truth in that statement. Aaron was an attractive guy, there was no doubt about that. But when he dressed up... he was irresistible.

But again, not the point. "You don't even know when the party is," I told him.

"Doesn't matter."

"It's tomorrow night." I held my breath, waiting for him to tell me that it was too short of notice and that he had other plans.

"Good deal. What time do I pick you up?" he asked.

"Can you really get a tux that quickly?" I blurted.

"Doll, I can do things mere mortals can't."

My breath escaped me in a rush. This had been far too easy for a last minute invite. I now had a date, and possibly a dress for a party that I didn't really want to go to in the first place. Things didn't generally work out that well for me.

Which left me wondering… just what was going to be the hiccup?

Chapter Eight

Payton

"Honey, I'm home!" I shouted to Chloe when I came through the front door around seven-thirty that night.

I'm not sure what had gotten into me, but ever since I hung up the phone with Aaron earlier in the day, I'd felt much better. Better than even before I had a party to worry about. We had shared texts for much of the afternoon, which had effectively distracted me from thoughts of the sexy mechanic. Aaron had sent me numerous selfies while he was out and about trying on tuxes. And yes, the man was right, he could do things mere mortals couldn't. He found a tuxedo, convinced the guy at the shop to give him a discount and was now set and ready to go.

I had been conversing with Chloe as well, mainly because Aaron and I were trying to work on what color cummerbund he should get — something he insisted on. Chloe suggested silver and that had me curious as to what she had found in her closet for me. Silver? If she put me in a silver dress, I was going to look like a glittery blow up doll, I was sure.

"What did you get for dinner?" Chloe hollered from her bedroom.

"Tacos." I resisted the urge to storm her room and see what she'd picked out; instead, I made a beeline for the table, setting the paper bag down before depositing my purse and my computer bag in my bedroom and kicking off my heels.

"You're an angel, you know that?" Chloe exclaimed when she joined me in the kitchen, throwing her arms around me from behind and hugging me.

I stilled instantly. Angel.

"You okay?" Chloe asked, making her way around me to the table.

"Fine. Is Aaron home yet?" I asked, her statement still ping-ponging around in my head. Angel. That was what Sebastian had called me.

Strange.

Shaking off the recurring sense of déjà vu, I blinked twice and forced my feet to move.

"Aaron's in his room with Mark," Chloe announced loudly in a singsong voice.

The door to Aaron's room flew open and there stood Mark in all of his handsome glory. Blond hair, blue eyes, built like a swimmer — which he was, so it kind of made sense.

"Hey, pretty girl," Mark greeted me as he made his way down the short hall. When he reached me, he pulled me into his arms and hugged me tightly.

"Hey. I hope you like tacos."

"Girl, I like anything you bring me. But I hope you brought enough."

Did I mention that Mark ate a lot? He said it had to do with all the swimming. He must swim an awful lot because he ate like a horse and never gained an ounce.

"Come on, pokey, dinner's here!" Mark called to Aaron down the hall.

"What do y'all want to drink?" I asked Chloe and Mark as I leaned into the refrigerator and rummaged around for a diet drink. We didn't usually keep them in the house, mainly because Chloe and I would devour them within a day, but I knew I'd hidden a couple in the back. Before anyone could answer, I retrieved the two cans and then held them up so she could see.

Chloe squealed.

Easily excitable, like I said.

"We'll take water." Aaron sounded snubbed as he came over to me and hugged me from behind.

"Don't act like you're upset. You don't drink sodas."

He hadn't had a soft drink in at least five years. I envied his will-power, I did. But I wasn't giving up my Diet Dr. Pepper for anyone.

Aaron retrieved two bottles of water from the refrigerator and then returned to the small breakfast nook where Mark was pulling out the chairs, waiting for Chloe and me to take our seats.

"Thank you." I smiled at Mark as I slipped into my chair, then glanced over at Chloe and added, "Please tell me you found a dress."

She'd already snatched the bag of tacos and was pouring the contents out onto the table.

"Why do you doubt me?" she asked, pretending to be offended.

"I don't. I'm just—"

Chloe interrupted me, her green eyes twinkling. "You're just eating. And then we'll try on the dress."

"Maybe we should try it on *before* I eat. I don't want to be bloated," I told her seriously, my eyes watching for her reaction. "The dress may not fit."

Mark and Aaron laughed while Chloe erupted in a fit of giggles. I sat there staring at the three of them, trying to keep a straight face. "What is so funny?"

"Just eat and tell us about your day," Chloe replied when she stopped laughing.

"Mine was boring," Aaron offered when no one spoke. "You?" He turned to Mark.

"Yep, just as boring."

All eyes turned to me.

"I went to Mr. Trovato's house today," I blurted before thinking.

I kept my attention on my taco, avoiding eye contact with the other three people at the table, but I could feel their gazes boring into me.

When no one said anything, I slipped my eyes up to Chloe's face.

Her eyebrow was cocked and she had stopped chewing. "I knew I should be worried."

It was my turn to laugh. "It wasn't like that."

"Spill," Mark said as he finished off his first taco. "He's rich, right? Nice house?"

"I don't know. I just saw the outside."

"And?"

"It's a house." I tried to sound indifferent. I seriously doubted Conrad Trovato's home could be classified as a mere house, but that wasn't the point of my story. "Anyway. He left his cell phone at home and his wife couldn't bring it to him. He told me to go. I went. No cell phone."

"What?" Aaron looked thoroughly confused. "Where was it?"

I laughed, realizing how Aaron had taken my statement. "I didn't get it." Without hesitating, I spewed the rest of the story, including the part about meeting the sexy as sin mechanic, never stopping to breathe.

"A mechanic? Are you serious?" Chloe asked, her eyes locked with mine.

I nodded, sipping my Diet Dr. Pepper.

"How hot are we talking? Lukewarm? Or like scorch-your-fingertips-if-you-touch-him hot?" Mark asked.

"The second one," I answered, studying my taco.

I knew I shouldn't have said anything. Chloe would constantly remind me of the mechanic from here on out and Aaron would be worried about me. It was a known fact that I didn't date much. And it wasn't because men didn't ask me out. They did. But I was a firm believer in the physiological reaction that I knew existed, even if I'd never felt it before. Until I found that, I wasn't interested in wasting any more time with guys who just didn't do it for me.

My hand stilled halfway to my mouth.

I'd felt that reaction to Sebastian, hadn't I?

Shaking off the unruly thought, I forced the taco to my mouth, taking a bite and ignoring the sensations that stirred in my belly when I thought about him.

I shouldn't have even brought him up. I didn't want to think about Sebastian, much less have someone ask me questions about him. I doubted I'd ever see him again and that… that kind of bugged me.

I managed to deflect the rest of their questions until finally we were finished eating. Before I could grab the taco wrappers to toss them in the trash, Chloe sprang up from her chair and grabbed my arm, dragging me into her bedroom before I realized we were on the move.

"We'll just… clean the kitchen," Aaron called, laughing.

"Thank you!" I hollered back, stumbling behind Chloe.

There on her bed was the sexiest dress I'd ever seen.

And the good news was that it wasn't silver. It was black.

"What do you think?" she asked, her hand pressed firmly to my back as she urged me closer to the dress.

"It's… It's… Wow. It's beautiful." That was an understatement. "It's also nearly nonexistent, Chloe."

"Not true. Try it on."

Yeah, it was safe to say that *little* was the most-prominent adjective in that little black dress. I grabbed the hanger and held it up in front of me.

"Try. It. On," Chloe commanded.

I could tell she was losing her patience, so I did as she asked. I carried the dress to my bedroom, slipped off my sweater and my skirt and then pulled the slinky, form-fitting dress on.

"This bra's not gonna work!" I shouted from my bedroom as I stood staring at the woman in the mirror.

The dress... Wow. It really was incredible. The kind of incredible that acted as camouflage, hiding all of those little things I hated about my body.

"Holy shit." Chloe whistled when she walked into the room, stopping to stand beside me as I continued to stare at myself in the mirror. "Yep, that'll work."

I reached for the hem of the skirt and tried to modestly pull it down to cover more of my thighs.

"Quit that," Chloe snapped as she slapped at my hand. "It's perfect just like that."

I met her gaze in the mirror and then glanced at the bra strap that was showing.

"Okay, maybe not perfect. But the bra we can fix. Worst case, go without one."

"Chloe!" I exclaimed. "You can't be serious." She *couldn't* be serious.

"You don't need a bra," she told me, reaching out and cupping my breast.

I slapped her hand away and laughed. "I do, too." I might not be well endowed, but I still needed a bra.

"Are you decent?" Aaron called from the living room.

"As decent as we'll ever be," Chloe bellowed.

The next thing I knew, Aaron and Mark were standing side by side in my doorway staring at me.

"Holy shit," Aaron said softly while Mark whistled.

"What?" I asked. "What's wrong?"

"Girl, that dress is fucking hot."

"I think it's the girl *in* the dress that's hot," Chloe corrected.

"That, too."

Aaron's eyes continued to rake over me. I waited for him to meet my gaze.

"What shoes are you gonna wear?" Mark asked. I glanced over to see his eyes trailing down to my bare feet.

Crap. Shoes.

"This we got," Chloe assured me. "We do wear the same size shoes." She practically skipped out of my bedroom, her ponytail bobbing merrily behind her.

I waited not so patiently, perusing my figure in the mirror while Chloe disappeared. Aaron flopped onto my bed and watched me while Mark continued to stand in the doorway.

"What's the party for?" Aaron asked, his hands behind his head, his long, lean body draped across my bed. He really was a good looking man. Blond hair, blue eyes, tall and trim, not bulky, but definitely well-built.

"Don't know. Mr. Trovato just invited me. I didn't ask what it was for."

"Maybe the mechanic will be there," Chloe said when she returned a second later, a pair of silver closed-toe heels dangling from her fingertips.

I snatched the shoes and glared at her. "He won't be there."

"How do you know?" Aaron asked, his blond eyebrows launching into his hairline.

"Because he's the mechanic," I offered, sounding not so sure of myself.

"Well, I'll cross my fingers for you." Chloe winked at me and then dropped onto the bed beside Aaron while I slipped the shoes on.

I continued to primp in the mirror while my best friends laughed and joked behind me. I lifted my hair up, let it drop down, wondering just how I should wear it. The entire time, I was thinking about Sebastian.

What if he was there? What would I say to him?

A renewed sense of nervousness overcame me. Could this be the shakeup that my life needed?

Or was I just getting my hopes up for nothing?

Chapter Nine

Sebastian

Dinner was a nightmare, just as I expected.

I should've gone out, or possibly nuked a frozen dinner at my house. If I had, I wouldn't have had to endure Conrad's wrath in front of my sister and my stepmother. Not that they weren't already familiar with our unique blend of dinner conversation.

Conrad was still harping on the fact that I'd sent Payton on her way without helping her to retrieve his cell phone. I found it amusing: both sending her on her way *and* listening to my father bitch about it.

Mighty fucking funny.

But, the fact that I wasn't taking him seriously had led to a conversation involving plenty of other transgressions that he wanted to call out until I could no longer taste the food I was eating.

Same story, different day.

I was a glutton for punishment. That was the only logical reason for why I put up with his shit. Sometimes I just didn't get it.

Ever since my mother died, I'd been going through the motions. Eleven years was a long damn time to muddle your way through life without having any particular reason for doing what you do. But that's where I was at in my head — lost. Completely and totally at the mercy of all the people around me.

Not that I wanted anyone to feel sorry for me. I'd made my own bed so to speak. By the time I was thirteen, I'd done time in juvie, and since then I'd talked my way out of a shitload of trouble, as well. My motto was that rules were meant to be broken, and I had always aimed to be the best I could be, so that's what I'd done. Ignoring the rules had become my benchmark for success. The more rules I could bend or break, the more successful I was.

Growing up, I didn't have much. My mother and I lived in a one bedroom apartment, which was sparsely furnished with mostly hand me downs from her older sister. My mother busted her ass to take care of me, even though she was incredibly young — only seventeen when she had me — and barely able to take care of herself. Her parents kicked her out when she told them she was pregnant, and they didn't offer to help even when we needed it most. We lived paycheck to paycheck and the worst part about it all, I had never been old enough to get a job and help out before she died. I'd tried though, working in a couple of mechanic shops for cash, but I never brought home enough money to make a difference.

Child support was nonexistent. In order to get child support, your mother had to do something to make that happen. Rachelle didn't want to have anything to do with Conrad Trovato. The most she'd taken from him was his last name when she put it on my birth certificate. And she'd regretted that every day after.

And as a way of saying thank you for not fucking up his entire life, Conrad pretended I didn't exist. He pretended my mother didn't exist.

Good ol' Conrad Trovato. My mother had been head over heels for him, and the bastard had turned his back on her. Then again, he'd been married to his first wife, Judy something or other, at that time and he was already making a name for himself. It wouldn't have gone over well if he admitted to having an illegitimate child with an underage girl.

Yep. Conrad had been twenty-six and married when he impregnated my seventeen-year-old mother. Needless to say, the two of them hadn't been all that concerned with morals and values when they decided to get together. Or protection, obviously.

Not only had Conrad built a company that afforded him the luxuries he had today, but he also came from old money. Money on top of money. I would never understand it.

But when Conrad attempted to pay my mother for her silence, Rachelle told him to go to hell and kept his secret for free.

That's where she and I differed. I would have taken the asshole's money and exploited him. Break the rules; that was the name of the game.

Every damn time I looked at him, I wanted to break his nose.

Tonight, after putting up with his tirade for a couple of minutes, I had hurried through the meal, excusing myself without his permission and hiding out in the garage attached to the guesthouse. This one was mine, the one place I spent hours and hours alone. It gave me time to think, which wasn't necessarily a good thing sometimes.

As though they knew I didn't need to be left to my own devices, ten minutes after I'd started tinkering with my Camaro, Leif and Toby showed up. My two closest friends tried to convince me to go out to the sports bar that we generally went to on Thursday nights, but I declined. I had too much shit to do — which translated to: *I didn't want to be around people.*

They were my closest friends and it was true, when I wasn't working, I was usually hanging with them. That's what friends did.

After I had refused to go out, Leif and Toby decided to stick around, snatching two beers from the refrigerator and planting their asses on the tailgate of my truck. We were talking about the new big block engine I was working on when my father made an appearance.

Standing to my full height, I put my hand on the edge of the Camaro's open hood and stared at him.

"I wanted to make sure you were planning to be at the party tomorrow night," Conrad stated in that authoritative tone that he generally used on his employees.

He almost made it sound as though I had a choice. I knew better.

"Busy. But y'all should have a grand ol' time," I replied sarcastically, glancing back at the engine.

"You will be there."

That's more like it. I knew it hadn't been a request.

"Why? Why the hell would you even want me there?" I turned my full attention on him then, noticing out of the corner of my eye that Leif and Toby were watching us intently.

"I want to unveil the new concept car."

"It's not ready," I informed him, as though he didn't already know that.

"But it will be."

"Not by tomorrow it won't," I argued.

"Maybe not. But it will be soon. I want to announce it, see if we have any potential buyers."

I should have been used to this shit. It wasn't the first time Conrad pushed a deadline on me. In return, he should have realized by now that the harder he pushed, the harder I pushed back.

"I'm busy."

"You'll be there," he repeated more sternly.

I could see the discomfort on Leif's and Toby's faces and I knew that I needed to chill. My father and I were notorious for going to blows whenever we engaged in conversation and more than once, my friends had been caught in the crossfire. I knew how uncomfortable it was. Hell, I lived this life. No one knew it better than me.

"Fine," I snapped, dropping the hood on the Camaro as a punctuation mark on my temper.

"Black tie. Seven o'clock."

I nodded, keeping my mouth shut for fear of what I might say. I didn't want to go to one of his stupid fucking parties. I didn't want to be anywhere near the assholes that he called friends. A few people knew who I was, but the rest of them had no clue. How Conrad had managed to do that all these years, I still didn't know. I didn't want to know.

If I had to guess, he had paid them off the same way he paid me off. At fourteen, when they were laying your mother in the ground and throwing dirt over her casket, you did what you had to do to survive. You see, my mother died in a car accident. She was T-boned by a drunk driver, or so the story went. Since the driver had fled the scene, no one really knew that to be true. She died on impact, and after losing her, I hadn't been right in the head.

Still wasn't.

I survived the overwhelming grief of losing the only person who loved me by blackmailing Conrad Trovato.

A paternity test proved that he was my father, although part of me had always hoped my mother had been wrong. Considering he was the only man she'd been with before I was born, it was a little difficult for her to make that shit up.

I'd been backed into a corner with only two options. The state would take me, or my father would. I chose option B, which at the time seemed like the lesser of two evils. I still questioned my decision sometimes.

Conrad hadn't been happy with the threat, but he eventually saw the light. That didn't mean that he didn't hate me. I was pretty sure he did.

I didn't fucking care.

"Awesome. You get to put on the penguin suit." Toby's roaring laughter yanked me away from my negative thoughts.

I darted my eyes toward the door, but my father was gone.

"Fuck off. Shut your face or I'll make you come with me."

"Bullshit." Toby recoiled as though I'd hit him with a cattle prod. "You ain't gonna get me anywhere near those people. What if that shit's contagious?"

"What shit?" Leif asked, sipping his beer and peering over at Toby.

"That hoity-toity shit. Man, I don't wanna walk around like I've got somethin' stuck up my ass, thank you very much."

"Too late for that," Leif offered, amused.

I laughed. I couldn't help myself.

Toby was a country boy to the core. He didn't have an issue speaking his mind. He was polite as hell around most people, but when it was just the three of us, he didn't hold back.

"Will his assistant be there?"

I snapped my head over to look at Leif. "What are you talking about?"

"I saw her on television, man. She's pretty fucking hot if you ask me," Leif replied.

"No one asked you," I snarled, remembering that my father had mentioned a spur of the moment press conference he'd held earlier that afternoon. That had to be what Leif was referring to.

"Defensive much?" Toby asked with a bellowing laugh.

"Fuck off."

"Man, you need to get laid. You keep making offers, but ain't no one here taking you up on them."

I flipped Leif off as I headed to the refrigerator and grabbed a beer. Dropping onto the couch in the corner, I crossed my legs at the ankle and reclined against the armrest.

As I closed my eyes, my mind drifted back to Payton, thanks to Leif's comment. I wondered whether she would be at the party. That snotty bitch Jasmine had always been invited to the parties my father threw. Didn't mean Payton would be there, but hell, it gave me something to look forward to.

"Why's your old man releasing the car now?" Leif asked, his voice coming closer to where I was sitting. I forced my eyes open, watching as he made his way to the sofa across from me. Toby wasn't far behind.

"Shit if I know," I answered. "He's been harping on me for a while now. I think he's hoping for seven figures on this one."

"Holy fuck," Toby exhaled sharply. "Seriously, man?"

"Yep. The last one went for just shy of a mil." Personally, I thought it could have gone for more, but my father caved at the last minute, accepting the highest of three offers.

I had to admit, the guy was pretty damn smart when it came to business, but his bargaining abilities needed some work.

"Did he let you take the car out?" Leif questioned, resting his big, beefy arm along the top of the other couch after planting his ass down on the leather.

"Nope." I had been willing to show them just what that car could do, but Conrad had refused, just as he always did.

No one knew that I took the car out anyway. Topped that motherfucker off at two-oh-nine on the track. Too bad no one had been there to see it. Not even Toby or Leif. As much as I wanted to brag about it, I never did. That was my thing, and if someone found out that I raced every car I worked on, I was pretty damn sure Conrad would put a tracking device on me just to keep tabs.

So I kept my mouth shut.

"Speakin' of racin'," Toby said in his good ol' boy drawl, leaning forward and resting his elbows on his knees as he pinned me with bright blue eyes.

"No one said anything about racing," I mumbled, smirking around my beer bottle.

"We're always talkin' about racin', man. Get with the program," Toby retorted. "There's a race. Two weeks from Saturday. Two large to get in, winner takes all."

"How many?" I inquired.

"Three so far. They're waitin' to see if you're game."

"You in?" Leif asked, as though he didn't already know the answer.

"I'm in," I assured him.

"Hot damn!" Toby yelled, grabbing his cell phone from his back pocket and shooting off a text.

It had been almost two months since the last race I was in. So far, over the course of the last two years, I'd gone unbeaten. To be fair to the other drivers, I used the Camaro mostly although I had a couple of other options. I'd dropped a fucking fortune in that car as it was and so far she hadn't let me down.

I took a long swallow of beer as I stared at the ceiling. I hadn't told Leif or Toby about the dream I'd had. The one that ended with the Camaro in a fireball with me trapped inside. I didn't think that was a subject anyone would want to talk about, so I'd kept it to myself.

Did it freak me out that I might die in one of the street races where there were no rules?

Sure.

Did I care?

No, not really.

I'd never had a reason to.

Chapter Ten

Payton

"Girl, we better get a move on," Aaron yelled from the living room.

I was standing in front of the full-length mirror in my bedroom, my eyes glued to the woman staring back at me. I recognized my dark hair, my dimpled chin, and my high cheekbones, but that was about it.

I looked… different.

Good different, but still different.

It was hard to believe that was me staring back from the glass, but the longer I stood there, the more I convinced myself that it was.

My hair was piled into some intricate design on top of my head thanks to Chloe and her wondrous abilities. A few pieces hung down, framing my face, which had been painted. I wasn't one to wear much makeup, so when Chloe offered to "do me up" as she put it, I'd been leery.

Surprisingly, she hadn't overdone it. My eyes had a smoky shadow on the lid, a thin black line along my lashes and black mascara on them, and a clear gloss on my lips to top it off. Nothing outrageous and I actually liked what I saw. I looked older, or at least I thought I did.

Silver hoops dangled from my ears while a silver chain hung around my neck, coming right above the swell of my breasts — made to appear bigger thanks to the push-up bra that I'd dug out of my drawer. I had forgotten all about that trip to the mall so long ago. I don't even remember what had prompted it, but I do remember spending an obscene amount of money in a lingerie store. Not that I'd ever had anyone to wear lingerie for, but at the time, I think I'd needed the boost of knowing I had something pretty on beneath my clothes.

It was certainly working now.

The sheer black thigh highs had been Chloe's suggestion. Personally, I thought they were an elegant touch, but I feared that if I sat down, the tops would be visible beneath the hem of the short black dress I was wearing. Chloe informed me that wasn't an issue. Whether she meant that they wouldn't show or that they would, I didn't know.

The closed-toe pumps were a nice touch, much classier than anything I owned.

"Here," Chloe said as she walked into my room holding out a small black clutch.

"Thanks. I'm not sure what I'd do without you," I told her, grabbing my cell phone and my lip gloss from my dresser and tossing them inside.

"Well, tonight you'd be going to a party naked."

True. I laughed, sparing myself one last look in the mirror.

"Here goes nothing."

I walked into the living room to find Aaron leaning against the wall and Mark fiddling with Aaron's bowtie. I stopped, momentarily stunned by how handsome he looked in his tuxedo. Sure, he'd been hot in high school, and had actually caused plenty of women to have heart palpitations at our senior prom, but this Aaron — older and wiser — was devastatingly handsome.

"Wow." The single word barely coming out.

"That's exactly what I said," Mark added. "Doesn't he look fucking hot?"

"I'll say."

Aaron offered me a sideways smirk before wrapping his hands around Mark's wrists and pulling him closer. I looked away when the two men kissed, not wanting to invade their privacy.

"Come on, you two. You can play kissy face later," Chloe told Mark and Aaron. "You kids are gonna be late," Chloe declared, urging me farther into the room. "I suggest you get going."

I glanced at the clock on the wall. It was already seven and we still had a forty-five minute drive ahead of us. That would put us at the party at the perfect time to be fashionably late. That is if I didn't stall any longer.

"Don't keep him out too late," Mark whispered to me as he offered a brief hug. "I'm going to take him home with me tonight and ravish him until dawn."

I blushed. I couldn't help it. It wasn't that I was a prude, but I could totally picture the two of them in my head and… well… I knew I shouldn't have been thinking about that.

Chloe handed me a silky black wrap and I slid it over my shoulders. It wouldn't do much against the chill in the November night air, but she had insisted it would look good.

Vain. That was obviously what I was going for tonight, I had told her, laughing.

"My car or yours?" I asked Aaron as I passed him on my way to the front door.

"Mine," he answered easily, reaching around me and opening the door.

Aaron was the best date ever. Probably because there weren't any expectations. We were friends and we could talk about anything and everything, which we did. From the moment we got into the car, until we pulled up to the guard station at Mr. Trovato's estate, there was never a lull in the conversation.

That changed when we pulled into the circular drive in front of Mr. Trovato's house.

"Holy shit," Aaron whispered as he peered through the windshield of his fancy little Honda with Bluetooth and satellite radio.

"Yep, that's what I thought the first time I saw it," I told him.

Granted, the place looked even more extravagant at night. Lights were hidden in the landscape, strategically placed to show off all of the details of the mansion. There was a line of expensive cars along one side of the driveway and several men scattering in all directions, probably moving the cars to a safer place.

A valet came over and opened my door for me, helping me out with a firm hand. I could have sworn he eyed me up and down a couple of times, but I pretended not to notice, although the sideways glance did wonders for my ego.

Aaron was instantly by my side offering me his arm and walking me toward the steps that led to the front door. A man in a suit — wielding a gun on his hip and an earpiece in his ear — greeted us before opening the front door and stepping back so we could enter.

I tried my best not to gape at what I saw next, but that was rather difficult to do.

Mr. Trovato's house was impressive on the outside, but on the inside it was... I wasn't even sure how to explain it. It looked like something straight out of the Roman Empire. Or so it did to me. Not that I'd seen any Roman empires, but if I had, this was what I imagined they would look like.

There were thick white columns that went at least twenty feet in the air on both sides, framing the circular entryway, three on each side. The floor looked like marble. It was a beautiful, gleaming white swirled with darker tones. An enormous sculpture of a semi-nude woman stood in the center of the entry, flanked by two grand staircases that circled up to the second floor. Somehow I managed not to whistle the way Chloe always did, but I had to say I was impressed.

"May I take your coat, madam?"

I turned to see another man in a suit, this one significantly older than anyone else I'd met so far. He looked like the same man I'd seen on the front steps the other day. I nodded, and he assisted in pulling the wrap from my shoulders before disappearing.

Another man, who looked a lot like Gun Guy by the front door, made his way over to us. "Right this way."

I glanced up at Aaron, lifting my eyebrows in a silent "Can you believe this?" He smirked back at me, looking regal and handsome and totally at ease. As though he actually belonged in a place like this.

I, however, did not feel like I belonged. I was suddenly self-conscious, wondering what other people thought when they looked at me. Was my skirt too high? Could they see the tops of my stockings when I walked? Did I look like a prostitute?

I didn't have time to ponder those questions for long though because we were on the move again, Aaron leading me as we followed behind the man in a dark suit. He took us deeper into the house, through what appeared to be a formal living room decked out with modern, white furniture that looked like it had never been used, and then down a hallway. At the end of the hall, we went up a different staircase, this one just as grand as the ones near the front door with its intricate iron railing, to the second floor and then down another long, wide hallway. By the time we arrived at our destination, I was thoroughly lost. When we came upon a set of double doors, he stopped, opened one of the doors and gestured us inside.

Holy. Smokes.

I didn't stumble, and I'm not sure how I managed that. Aaron and I walked into an enormous ballroom filled with people. A waiter was standing near the door holding a tray of champagne flutes. Because social protocol demanded that I do so, I took one of the flutes, as did Aaron before we made our way inside.

Social protocol probably didn't demand that I down the champagne in two swallows, but I did that anyway.

"How much money does this guy have? And why the hell didn't he hire a better decorator?" Aaron asked, his voice a mere breath against my ear.

Laughing and gently elbowing him in the ribs, I answered with, "A lot."

I didn't know what that number was, but obviously it was enough, and Aaron did have a point. Although nice, the place felt a little stuffy to me. A little too upper crust.

The walls donned a fancy gold and red wallpaper with thick white trim framing it. The floor was dark hardwood, with plush red carpet outlining the room. There were large gilded plaques of various designs hanging above the doors and heavy gold drapes covering the floor to ceiling windows.

Suffice it to say, it did suit Mr. Trovato.

I spent the next few minutes taking everything in. From the sophisticated décor to the fancy gowns on the women and the expensive tuxes on the men. As I figured, most of the people I encountered were older, and just as I thought, everyone seemed to look right past me. If it hadn't been for a man who had bumped into me and politely apologized, I would have believed that I was invisible.

"Hey," a chipper female voice sounded from behind me and I turned, coming face to face with… "You must be Payton. I'm Aaliyah. Welcome to my humble abode."

Aaron snorted.

"I like you already," Aaliyah said to Aaron. "And you are?"

"Aaron." He offered Aaliyah his traffic stopping smile. "Payton's gay best friend who was wrangled into attending."

Aaliyah's grin was radiant, as was the rest of her. She stood just a few inches taller than me, her long, blond hair curled and hanging down her back. The dress she wore probably cost more than I made in a year and it fit her like a glove, the turquoise color setting off her bright blue eyes and olive complexion perfectly.

"I definitely like him," she whispered to me. "Don't worry. It's not as bad as it looks."

"Really?" Aaron asked skeptically making a production out of looking around, earning him another laugh from Aaliyah.

"Okay, it's as bad as it looks. But stick around, things usually get exciting later on."

"Exciting? As in the old people get naked and dance on the tables?" Aaron questioned.

Aaliyah gave my arm a gentle squeeze and laughed. "God, I hope not."

"It's very nice to meet you," I told Aaliyah, grinning at Aaron's joke.

"You, too. I'm sorry I wasn't here yesterday. I had an early class and if I'm late anymore, I'm gonna get in serious trouble."

"No worries," I assured her. I didn't bother to mention to her my interaction with Sebastian, although I wanted to ask her who he really was.

"You two have fun. I'll catch up to you later." Aaliyah gave my arm another friendly squeeze and then walked a few feet away, greeting one of the older couples.

"Mr. Trovato's daughter," I explained to Aaron.

"I figured as much."

"How so?"

"She's probably the youngest person in the place, and though I think your boss probably has a mistress or two, I didn't figure her to be that young."

"He does *not* have a mistress." I slapped Aaron lightly on the arm. I sure hoped Conrad didn't have a mistress.

"Don't be so sure of that." The deep, rumbling voice came from behind me.

I spun around so fast, I nearly dropped my empty champagne flute, but Sebastian retrieved it and set it on a passing waiter's tray like he did that sort of thing every day.

I merely stared at him, a strange tingle igniting deep in my core as I came face to face with the man I'd met just yesterday. The guy from my dream. The mechanic. He looked significantly different than the last time I saw him though. Tonight he wasn't sporting tattered jeans. No, tonight he was wearing a tuxedo and likely garnering the attention of every woman in the place.

The guy made a pair of worn, tattered jeans look incredible, but he wore a tuxedo better than any man I'd ever met.

As we stood there, motionless, neither of us said anything for a few heartbeats. My pulse was racing and if it hadn't been for Aaron's warm hand on my back, I probably would have forgotten where I was.

Sebastian peered over my shoulder at Aaron and I thought I saw a flash of anger glitter in his beautiful golden eyes, but it was gone as fast as it had come, leaving me to think I was imagining things.

"Enjoy the party, Angel," Sebastian whispered, nodding his head at me, our eyes locking briefly.

He didn't linger. He continued walking right past me without looking back.

"Who was that?" Aaron turned at the same time I did, so that he could follow Sebastian with his eyes.

"No one," I murmured.

Mechanic, my ass.

Chapter Eleven

Payton

Two hours into the party, and I was wondering when the fun was going to start. I'd managed to drink six flutes of champagne and was starting to feel the effects of the alcohol, although that hadn't helped to alleviate the nerves that were attacking my insides. Aaron had forced me to eat some of the hors d'oeuvres, which was probably the only reason I wasn't flat on my face at this point.

My head was beginning to hurt from looking around the room, trying to locate Sebastian at every turn. Ever since our brief run-in, I hadn't seen him again, but I could feel his presence. I knew he was there somewhere.

"Care to dance?" Aaron stopped me from taking another flute from a passing waiter.

I glared at him in warning. That earned me a smile.

"No, I do not want to dance," I slurred, but he just took me in his arms and led me to the center of the room.

"You're drunk."

"I am not," I argued, knowing full well that I was. I wasn't much of a drinker, aside from a beer or two every now and again. I didn't even like champagne, yet tonight I'd been drinking it like water.

"Whatever you say, doll," Aaron replied, pressing his hand to the back of my head and forcing my face to rest against his chest. He was holding one of my hands and I slid my other hand beneath his jacket, clutching his back. It probably looked intimate, but I was trying to keep from sliding to the floor and letting sleep take over. That, and being with Aaron made me feel safe.

He pressed his lips against the top of my head as we danced around the room, the music soft and slow. The lights had dimmed a short while ago and most of the couples had migrated to the dance floor, too. As we moved, I closed my eyes, willing my brain to stop spinning.

Aaron must have realized the effect the dancing was having on my inebriated state because he slowed even more, our feet barely moving.

"Who was the guy from earlier?" Aaron asked, his voice low, soothing.

"I told you. No one."

"Right. And I didn't believe you. That's why I asked again. Who is he?"

"The mechanic," I informed him, hating the fact that the alcohol was making my lips flap when they shouldn't.

"Ahh. That explains it."

"I don't think he's the mechanic," I admitted.

I could hear Aaron's gruff chuckle against my ear. I amused him. I knew I did.

I amused a lot of people these days.

"Who do you think he is?"

"No idea," I told him, digging my fingernails into his back. I really didn't want to talk.

Aaron apparently took the hint because we spent the next few minutes slow dancing until the music disappeared. At first I thought I'd fallen asleep standing up, but then a voice came over the sound system and the lights went out, pitching the room into complete darkness.

An automated voice started talking and several strobe lights began alternating to the bass that kicked in. What happened next was straight out of a movie. Seriously, I was pretty sure I'd seen it before in a movie. I don't remember which one though.

I stayed close to Aaron while the robotic voice rambled on about engines and cars and speed while a series of lights drew designs along one of the walls. There were gasps and clapping and then the lights came up to reveal a car sitting in the middle of the room.

"Impressive," Aaron stated dryly. "I'm pretty sure that's been done before."

Another waiter approached and while Aaron's attention was snagged by the fancy sports car, I grabbed another flute and downed it in one gulp.

I really didn't like champagne; tonight's sampling only solidified that for me.

"You better slow down," Aaron stated firmly when he turned to look at me.

I didn't argue. There was no point. I just wanted to go home. I'd already been there for more than two hours and Mr. Trovato hadn't even greeted me, although I'd seen him at least three times and I was pretty sure he'd seen me as well.

I don't know if he was purposely ignoring me or if it was just my imagination, but I was beginning to get frustrated. As it was, the only person who'd spoken to me all night, besides Aaron, was Aaliyah.

Sebastian didn't count.

"We need to get you some water."

Water was good.

Aaron was escorting me away from the crowd when a wave of nausea hit me. "I… I need to use the restroom," I told him hurriedly.

"I'll take you," he replied softly, taking my arm.

"No," I insisted, pulling back from him. "I'll… I'll be right back."

I needed some air and I didn't want Aaron following me in the event that I did get sick. I met his gaze and waited until he nodded. His eyes met mine briefly, but then I took off for the door. Out in the hall, the sound of my heels on the marble floor made my ears ring, but then blessedly I was on the carpet. When I stumbled once, sliding my hand along the wall to keep myself upright, I knew I'd had too much to drink. As the stairs came into view, I suddenly wondered just how I was going to safely make it down without falling on my face and rolling my way to the first floor.

I stopped at the top and peered down, taking a deep breath and trying to clear the fuzziness from my head. I'd walked down plenty of stairs in my life. Surely I could handle a few more.

A strong but gentle hand gripped my arm and I looked up, expecting to see Aaron standing behind me. My mouth fell open as I stared up into those glistening gold eyes that had haunted my every thought since meeting him yesterday.

Sebastian didn't say anything, but he didn't look away either. I could tell he was thinking about something, and I suddenly hoped he wasn't thinking about giving me a gentle nudge down the stairs. But then he grinned and every thought in my brain leaked right out.

Without saying a word, he urged me closer to the stairs, his hand sliding down around my waist as he held me close to him. With his reassuring grip on me, I managed to make it down the stairs without an ungraceful face plant and the next thing I knew, he was leading me out through a door at the back of the house, right onto a dimly lit veranda.

I was pretty sure just the patio area was bigger than my parents' entire backyard.

I kept my thoughts to myself as we continued to walk to a shadowy corner, away from a few people who were milling about.

"Thank you," I mumbled, unable to look at him when we stopped walking. I took deep, steadying breaths, willing myself under control. I was no longer queasy, but I was hot. The cool breeze did little to ease the heat that coursed just beneath my skin, but I shivered anyway.

"What are you thanking me for?" Sebastian chuckled, the deep baritone of his voice sending a chill dancing down my spine.

"For not letting me fall to my death down the stairs."

I placed my hands on the concrete railing that wrapped around the veranda, breathing slowly as I stared out into the darkness. The moon was out, casting a white glow on the trees, the moonbeam bouncing off a pond in the distance. My head was spinning, but I think it had more to do with the incredible scent of Sebastian's cologne than the alcohol.

Just as I had earlier, I felt his presence more than I saw him. He was standing just to my right, a step behind me which offered me a small measure of comfort. If he got too close, I feared what I might do. My body had taken on a mind of its own, ignoring all logical instruction from my brain. Being alone with Sebastian wasn't a good thing, at least not where my common sense was concerned.

I don't know how long we stood there, but I didn't move, didn't look at him. For some reason, I was scared to make a sound, not wanting him to leave. I knew he was still there beside me because I could smell him, hear his steady breathing.

I shivered when a gust of wind whipped behind the house, wrapping my arms around myself. But even if I froze to death, I didn't want to walk away. I don't know what it was about Sebastian, but I was drawn to him. Ever since we met yesterday, I'd thought about him endlessly. And now he was standing here, the silence between us surprisingly comforting, but at the same time unnerving.

He shifted, and I thought for a second that he was going to walk away, but then his jacket was resting on my shoulders, my senses overwhelmed by him. I closed my eyes as I inhaled, letting the rich, musky scent of his cologne seep into me while the residual warmth from his body heat enveloped me. I suddenly wished his arms were around me.

But I knew that was crazy talking.

Several minutes passed. I could hear a few people talking, a woman laughing. The music was muted outside, but I could still make out the slow, jazzy tune.

"Feeling better yet?" Sebastian's arm brushed against me as he moved closer to the rail, setting his empty beer bottle on the top.

"Much," I said a little too quickly, turning to face him.

Whether it was the alcohol or my own desire, I wanted to question him, to find out what that niggling was in the back of my mind. "Are you really a mechanic?" I asked bluntly, gripping his jacket closer to my body.

Sebastian took one step toward me. I took one step back, but my butt hit the concrete railing, effectively halting my getaway.

"I'm a mechanic," he stated, his voice low, seductive. He was looking into my eyes as though he could see right through me, as if he knew what I was thinking.

If he knew, I'd be mortified because right at that moment, I was thinking about kissing him. Wondering what his lips would feel like against mine, and if I would be able to taste beer on his tongue.

Sebastian's finger came up and traced a line down my cheek. I leaned into his touch, unable to resist. "What is it about you, Angel?" Sebastian asked, but I sensed that the question was rhetorical so I didn't answer.

I allowed my gaze to drop to his lips, willing him to move just an inch closer.

He did and our lips grazed one another's, his breath warm against my mouth. My eyes closed and I prayed he would kiss me, that he would do something to suppress the ache that had taken up residence between my thighs.

I'd never wanted a man the way I wanted Sebastian.

Never.

"Your boyfriend's probably looking for you." His voice was much lower than before, darker. I could practically sense the hunger in his tone.

I opened my eyes, drawing away from him slightly so I could see his face. My pulse was pounding furiously, my breath coming in rapid gasps. I wanted to say something, but the words didn't come.

So as I stood there memorizing the swell of his bottom lip and the ring that decorated it, the slight crook of his nose, the dark, thick lashes that framed his incredibly beautiful eyes, I didn't tell him that he was wrong. Aaron wasn't my boyfriend. I wasn't even the right gender for Aaron, but for some reason, I didn't want to correct Sebastian's assumption. I didn't know anything about him, other than he wasn't who he said he was. Sure, maybe he was a mechanic, but the fact that he was at a party, dressed to the nines in what I could only assume *wasn't* a rented tuxedo, looking every bit like a man who had money and wasn't put off by it, told me he hadn't been entirely truthful.

I didn't need that in my life. For whatever reason, Sebastian had felt the need to lead me on, to make me believe otherwise and although my body was set to slow boil when he was around, it wasn't in my best interest to acknowledge it. He was a bad boy. One I should run away from, not run toward.

And I was smarter than that.

Sebastian broke away, peering over his shoulder and I turned to see Aaron coming toward us.

"There you are," Aaron said softly, his eyes pinning Sebastian in place.

Aaron rarely looked angry, but as he glared at Sebastian, I could feel his ire. Why was he so pissed?

Without saying anything, Aaron worked his jacket off, pulled Sebastian's from my shoulders and handed it back to him before wrapping me in his warmth. He didn't say a word to Sebastian though and that was what made the moment so awkward.

"Let me take you home," Aaron suggested, putting his arm around me and pulling me against his side. I was tempted to push him away, to ask him what his problem was, but I was too shaken to do so.

"Good to see you, Payton." Sebastian's voice was still soft and seductive, almost as though he was keeping a secret from Aaron. "I look forward to seeing you again."

Oh, hell.

This was one of those testosterone contests. Who had the bigger balls and all that nonsense. I didn't respond, just nodded and leaned into Aaron a little.

When Aaron led me away from Sebastian, I was tempted to look back at him, wanting to know what he was thinking.

"Don't do it," Aaron muttered under his breath, his arm wrapping tightly around me.

"Do what?" I tilted my head back so that I could look up at him.

He just smiled as we walked inside.

We had just made it to the front door when Mr. Trovato came down the stairs.

"Payton," he called, causing me to turn toward him. "Leaving already?"

"Yes, sir," I said, just as Aaron said, "She's not feeling well."

"Well, thank you for coming. I hope you had a good time."

"I did," I lied. "Thank you for inviting me."

I felt a set of eyes watching me from across the room, and I looked past Mr. Trovato to see Sebastian leaning against the wall, his legs crossed at the ankles as he stared at me.

I quickly turned my attention back to my boss, but not before both Aaron and Conrad were looking over at Sebastian.

Conrad met my gaze again and I saw his irritation in the brown depths, but then it was masked quickly. "Take good care of her, son," he said to Aaron, sparing him a brief glance, then looking at me and adding, "And I'll see you on Monday."

Unable to speak through the desert that had taken up residence in my throat, I nodded my head and after receiving my wrap from the butler/man, I allowed Aaron to lead me outside. I managed, I still don't know how, not to look at Sebastian again.

The valet brought Aaron's car around quickly and I kept my mouth shut until we were safely inside before I punched Aaron in the arm. "Why did you do that?" I exclaimed.

Aaron laughed and rubbed his arm. "What did *I* do?"

"Why did you make Sebastian think we were together?"

Sure, I had allowed Sebastian to believe Aaron was my boyfriend, but it was something else entirely for Aaron to act so possessively.

"You've got a lot to learn, kiddo."

"Don't call me that," I shouted unnecessarily. "I'm older than you."

"By a minute." Aaron chuckled as the gates opened allowing us to leave the estate.

"By a month," I corrected him as I closed my eyes and rested my head against the back of the seat, snuggling into Aaron's jacket. "You still didn't answer me."

"Doll, you've got a lot to learn about men."

"Tell me about it." I was referring to the testosterone overload I'd been in the middle of just a few minutes ago. "In the meantime, why don't you enlighten me?"

"It's all in how you play the game," Aaron stated.

"I don't *want* to play the game," I retorted.

"We all play the game, doll."

"But thanks to you, Sebastian's gonna think I really do have a boyfriend."

"Maybe. But that's what you want."

I turned my head toward him and peered at him through one eye. "Why's that?"

"Because men want what they can't have. And, sweetheart, I just set the dominos in motion. Sebastian isn't gonna be able to stop thinking about you."

"Wait." I studied him briefly. "How do you know his name's Sebastian?"

Aaron chuckled, sparing me a sideways glance. "Because you just said it was."

"Oh." Closing my eyes, I returned to my original position, my head facing forward, eyes closed. "It doesn't matter anyway. It's not like I'm gonna see him again."

"Oh, honey, you'll see him again. Probably sooner rather than later."

The gentle hum of the tires on asphalt lulled me to sleep. As I drifted off, I didn't bother telling Aaron that I hoped he was right.

Chapter Twelve

Sebastian

I should have snuck back to the guest house when I'd had the chance. If I had, I wouldn't have just spent the last few minutes staring out into the darkness with a woman I knew I needed to stay away from. But the silence had been comforting, her presence even more so. I could've stood there all night, listening to her soft breaths, letting the spicy sweet scent of her perfume tease me.

She had all but dared me to kiss her. How I refrained, I still don't know. It had taken everything in me not to pull her against my body and crush my mouth to hers just to see if she tasted as sweet as I suspected she did. As it was, when my lips brushed hers, I'd nearly come like a fucking teenage boy.

I should've kissed her.

And then her boyfriend had shown up and ruined the moment. The chaos in my head returned the instant he stepped outside, as though whatever filter Payton provided had been interrupted. I don't know what it was, or whether I was just conjuring up crazy bullshit in my head, but I'd felt an overwhelming peace when I was near Payton tonight.

She calmed me, even when she wound me up at the same time.

I'd spent the last couple of hours watching her from the shadows of the ballroom, not wanting her to know I was there. It had been hell on earth watching her laugh, talk and dance with the tall guy who'd arrived with her. At one point, I had envisioned shooting out his kneecaps just because he was with her and I wasn't.

My sister had come over briefly to talk, only to give me a hard time when she caught me watching Payton. Aaliyah had a huge grin on her face when I asked her about the guy Payton was with, having seen the three of them talking shortly after Payton arrived. She informed me that his name was Aaron, and she went on and on about how funny he was and how cute the two of them were together.

I knew her well enough to see through her. She'd been trying to get a rise out of me, but it hadn't worked.

Little witch.

But now Payton was leaving with the blond guy and my night had officially gone to shit.

"Sebastian."

I rolled my eyes at the sound of Conrad's voice. I could hear the click of his Italian loafers on the marble floor as he approached. Slowly, I transferred my gaze from the front door over to Conrad's face.

"Stay away from her," he commanded, his voice rough, his eyes beady.

"What?" I twisted to face him as I stood to my full height. We were nose to nose and I was tempted to punch him in his fucking mouth. I hated when he treated me like a goddamn child.

"You heard me," he growled quietly. "Stay the fuck away from her."

"Or what?" I taunted.

"Don't push me, Sebastian. She's off limits to you. Do you understand? I'm not gonna sit by and let you ruin her."

Ruin her?

What the fuck.

I laughed, but there wasn't an ounce of humor in it. "Right. 'Cause that's what I do. I ruin women." I took a step closer, our noses nearly touching as I narrowed my eyes on him. "I'm not you. I don't use them and throw them away. That's your M.O. Not mine. And if you know what's good for you, you'll take your threats elsewhere, old man."

Conrad didn't back down, but I saw a glimmer of fear in his brown eyes. He knew not to push me. I had a fragile grasp on my temper most of the time as it was. He knew that.

Realizing we'd gained an audience, Conrad took a step back just as I turned to walk away. When he put his hand on my arm, it took every ounce of willpower I possessed not to turn around and nail him between the eyes with my fist. I glanced down at where he was gripping my arm tightly, then back up to his face.

"I'm serious, Sebastian."

I shrugged his hand off. "So am I."

With that, I turned and walked away. I noticed Aaliyah was watching me from across the room, her eyes wide. She'd seen Conrad and I go toe to toe before, but just as I did, she knew that one of these days I was going to lose it.

That, or I was going to implode.

Half an hour later I was in my workout room, *Holler Til You Pass Out* by *3OH!3* blaring from the speakers, sweat pouring from my face as I pummeled the heavy bag hanging from the ceiling. The bass reverberating off the walls matched the pounding in my skull and the throbbing in my knuckles.

While I threw one punch after another, gasping for air as I exhausted my muscles, I pictured Conrad's face on the bag.

This was my stress reliever, something I relied on to keep me sane. That and racing. Those were the only two things that helped to quiet the voices in my head, to calm the fury that pounded in my blood.

I stopped moving, my chest heaving as I wrapped my arms around the bag, trying to keep from falling to the floor.

My thoughts immediately drifted to Payton.

She had calmed me in a way I'd never known before. In a way that no amount of punching a faceless enemy or redlining a powerful engine to its breaking point ever could.

For as long as I could remember, I'd battled the fury that was a living, breathing thing inside me. Chaos was how I referred to it. A constant state of chaos that had a stranglehold on me.

Stay away from her.

My father's words invaded my thoughts, a red haze clouding my vision momentarily.

In all the time that I'd known the man, after all the warnings he had dished out, all of the threats he made, never had I wanted to defy him so badly.

But for the first time, it wasn't to get back at him.

It had nothing to do with him period.

I wanted Payton. I wanted her with a passion I'd never experienced before. I wanted to hold her in my arms, to lay her out beneath me and bury myself so deep inside her that she no longer thought about any other man. I wanted to own her, to possess her.

It was crazy.

I was crazy.

Pushing away from the heavy bag, I retrieved the bottle of water sitting on the window sill. Staring out into the night, I could see my reflection on the window glass. The crazed look in my eyes was something I'd gotten familiar with. I knew what was inside of me. A beast that needed to get out.

No amount of adrenaline had ever extricated the turmoil though, and Lord knows I had tried. Too many times.

I downed the rest of the water and tossed the bottle into the small recycle container in the corner. Placing my hands on the wall above the window, I leaned forward, trying to see past the reflection into the night and that's when it came back to me.

Payton.

The dreams.

It was her I'd seen, even before I met her.

She was the one I'd been drawn to, the reason I hadn't wanted to wake up. Closing my eyes, I tried to conjure up the image of the woman who infiltrated my dreams, the way she looked then. She was just out of reach.

Just like Payton.

Stay away from her.

As Conrad's words bounced around in my head and images of Payton's face continued to drift through my mind, I knew what the right thing to do was.

For her sake, I needed to stay away. I needed to pretend we never met, ignore the fact that I was obsessed with her.

There was only one problem.

She unhinged me.

And I wasn't strong enough to resist her.

Chapter Thirteen

Sebastian

One week later
Thursday

Wiping the sweat from my face with the edge of my T-shirt, I allowed the wrench to fall from my hand and land with a shrill clatter on the concrete floor. The sound was surprisingly reminiscent of the noise that was clanging inside my head. Even with the music blasting, I couldn't block out the frenzied thoughts bouncing around inside my skull.

The garage door was open, the chilly November wind whipping through the open space, but it did little to cool me down. My skin felt hot, my blood was racing through my veins. Although I could usually get myself under control by working, that wasn't even helping today.

"Fuck," I growled, thrusting my hands through my hair, then sliding them down to the back of my neck.

I paced the floor just like that, my eyes on the ground, my hands gripping my neck, the muscles pinched tight.

I'd been strung tight as a bow since last Friday. Six days ago.

The last time I saw Payton.

I could still feel her breath on my lips. I was kicking myself in the ass for not kissing her, for not taking her into my arms and holding her, touching her. I just wanted to know what she would feel like against me. If I could have done anything differently about that night, that would have been it. It was the only damn thing I could think about.

And it was slowly killing me.

It didn't help that Conrad was watching me like a hawk. If I didn't know better, I would have thought he was tracking me. Maybe he was. I actually wouldn't be at all surprised.

If it weren't for my sister requesting that I have dinner with them every night, avoiding him would have been a hell of a lot easier. But it was hard for me to say no to Aaliyah. So, every night, I had to endure my father's scowl at the table. He would purposely bring up Payton's name and every damn time his eyes would be on me. So far, not since the night of the party, he hadn't warned me to stay away from her, at least not verbally, but I knew he was thinking it. I could tell by that tell-tale gleam in his eyes that he was just waiting for me to defy him.

Just so we're entirely clear, I fully intended to defy him, but it had nothing to do with getting back at him. Not this time.

From the moment Payton walked out the front door with that blond guy, the noose had continued to tighten around my neck and it wasn't easing up. The longer I waited before seeing her again, the more frustrated I was becoming.

I had dreamed about her again. The night of the party. I don't know if it was because I'd been thinking about her, or trying to decipher the original dream, but she'd appeared out of thin air. Waking up had been brutal. Reality could be a cold bitch sometimes.

Reaching down, I grabbed the wrench I'd discarded and as I was standing up, the music cut off suddenly and I heard someone clear their throat. I knew without looking who it was.

"Yes?" I asked my father, not bothering to look at him.

"I need an estimate on when you'll have that finished."

Yep. Just as I thought. He was there to ride my ass about the project, wanting me to be finished already. I'd told him a hundred times, I didn't know. He obviously wasn't accepting that answer.

"When I'm done," I told him honestly, tossing the wrench onto the toolbox, letting it clank against the other tools. Grabbing the grease rag, I wiped my hands as I turned to look at Conrad.

"Not good enough," he barked.

Holding my hands up in mock surrender, I smirked at him. "Have at it, old man. You wanna take a shot at making it work, do your worst. Or wait, better yet, why don't you get your guys over here, see what they can do with it."

He'd tried that before. Not that the guys he had working for him weren't good at what they did. They were. I was just better. It required a good ear to listen to a car, a steady hand to fine tune it, and I'd proven time and time again that no one could solve an issue better than I could.

I didn't bother to tell him that I was stalling on purpose. That wouldn't have gone over very well.

"Sebastian."

"Yes?" I feigned innocence. I was so fucking tired of this dance we were doing. Conrad could give two shits about when I had this prototype complete. I was pretty sure, after the spectacle he'd made at the party that someone was ready to throw a ton of fucking cash at him and he was just greedy.

As far as I was concerned, they could wait. And so could he.

"This is absurd." Conrad moved closer. He didn't get too close, probably worried he'd get grease on that pretty fucking shirt of his.

"You're tellin' me," I agreed. If he would stop breathing down my neck, we wouldn't have to go through this every damn day.

"You've got three days," he finally said, surprising the shit out of me.

I spun around to face him directly, trying to rein in my temper. "Excuse me?"

"You heard me. Three days. I want that damn thing finished by Monday. If it means you work through the weekend, so be it."

I could hear my teeth grinding together, feel the muscle in my jaw flexing.

"And if I don't agree?"

Conrad took a deep breath. "Then we'll have to have a discussion regarding our little arrangement."

"Good idea," I taunted as I took a step closer. He took one step back. "Why don't we do that, *Dad*? Why don't we just sit down and hash it out? Maybe call a press conference. I think the media would be thrilled to learn more about the man behind the fake fucking smiles and the fancy ass suits."

"Goddammit, Sebastian!" Conrad yelled, storming across the room and stopping abruptly, his back to me. "Why the fuck do you have to keep doing this? I've given you everything you could possibly want. Every goddamn thing and this is the thanks I get?"

I swallowed hard. "I'm sorry," I said facetiously when Conrad spun around. "I forgot about all the things you gave me. I was too busy remembering," I walked toward him, my voice lowering, "all the shit you took away from me."

Conrad glared, but he remained silent.

We were through here. There was nothing left to say. This was how it usually ended between us. A stalemate. He thought he could threaten me, but what he didn't realize was that I wasn't some dumbass fourteen-year-old kid anymore. I'd long outgrown my initial fear of being accepted by him. I didn't want his approval. I didn't need it.

"I've got to go back to the office," Conrad stated, as though that was the reason for the end of our conversation.

"Oh, one more thing." I waited until he turned to face me again. He cocked an eyebrow in question. "How's Payton?"

With that, Conrad spun on his expensive fucking heel and waltzed right out the door, leaving me standing there. All alone.

Just as I always was.

Chapter Fourteen

Sebastian

I ended up having dinner out that night, choosing not to face my father's wrath. I'd pushed him too far and I didn't want to deal with the repercussions. Not to mention, I didn't want to put Aaliyah through that either.

That and my curiosity was going to get the best of me if I had to listen to Conrad talk about Payton over dinner one more time. He would do it too, just to irritate me.

One of these days, I was going to lose my shit and it wasn't going to matter who ended up as collateral damage. Where Payton was concerned, I was a ticking time bomb. It was as though I needed my next fix. I was a junkie, an addict. I wanted a woman I knew very little about and no matter how hard I tried, I couldn't understand what the fuck it was about her that had me so obsessed.

I was slowly going crazy.

I wanted to know more about her. No, scratch that, I wanted to know *everything* about her. Where was she from? How old was she? What did she look like naked?

I was definitely interested in the last part.

So, instead of risking a slip of the tongue in front of my father, I was sitting at a sports bar, watching hockey and drinking beer with my two closest friends, Leif Connelly and Toby Brindle.

"Man, are you picturing some chick naked?" Leif questioned, lifting his beer bottle in my direction.

"I was thinkin' the same thing," Toby added in that slow, southern drawl that drew women like a magnet.

"Shut up, assholes," I mumbled, hating how well they knew me.

Okay, so yes, I was picturing Payton naked. Didn't mean I had to share my thoughts with anyone, let alone the two people who would harass me until I wanted to punch them in the face simultaneously.

"Who is she?" Leif asked.

"No one," I barked.

"Right. 'Cause '*no one*' makes you drool when you picture her naked," Toby inserted, smiling around the lip of his beer bottle.

"Did I mention you could… fuck off," I bit out, unable to keep from smiling.

It wasn't a secret that I didn't spend my time with many women. Oh, there'd been a few, sure. After all, I wasn't a saint. But nothing serious.

Not that I didn't find women fascinating, nor was it due to the fact that I didn't have my fair share of female attention. But I'd learned early on, thanks to who my family was, that women tended to see dollar signs when they found out where I lived. I didn't make a habit of bringing women to the estate, but there had been a handful. Needless to say, the caliber of female that I usually attracted were more interested in what they could get *from* me rather than what they could do *with* me. If that wasn't a turnoff, I don't know what was.

"So now you've got imaginary girlfriends? What the hell is this world coming to?" Leif razzed good-naturedly.

"Who the hell are you tryin' to kid?" Toby snorted. "He's always had imaginary girlfriends."

I knew Leif and Toby would give me a hard time. They always did. Didn't matter that Leif usually got the waterfall of women that I left in my wake or that Toby had his hands full on nearly a nightly basis. We were usually together, which meant when one girl arrived, there were normally two more not far behind. Sometimes more than that. Chicks loved Leif and Toby, which, according to them, were their reasons behind their playboy statuses.

I'd known Leif since I was fourteen, since my first day in a new school when I was pissed off and hated the world. Leif had been my saving grace, I guess you could say. He hadn't taken any of my shit when I wanted to do nothing more than fight with anyone who crossed my path. His ability to ignore my bullshit was the main reason we'd become friends. That and he was as much of an adrenaline junkie as I was. The only point of contention between the two of us was that he had the hots for my sister, something I wasn't particularly fond of. So far, I'd managed to keep the two of them apart, although it was getting harder and harder these days.

But I didn't want to think about Leif and Aaliyah. Not now. Not ever.

As for Toby, we met our freshman year of high school. I'd smoked him in a street race, but rather than threaten to kick my ass like a lot of assholes did, Toby shook my hand. We'd been friends ever since.

"She's not imaginary," I grumbled, sipping my beer. I rested my forearms on the table and picked at the label on my bottle, trying to keep my head down.

Leif twisted in his chair to face me directly. "So there *is* a girl?"

"Of course, there's a girl," Toby declared, looking not at all shocked.

"No," I lied. "Ain't no damn girl." No reason to get Leif all worked up. He was always giving me shit about dating. I tended not to do it by design.

"So, I saw your father on TV again today." Leif looked at me and then glancing over at Toby, mischief gleaming in his dark brown eyes.

I leaned back in my chair, tipping it onto two legs. While I watched Leif and Toby, I tilted my beer bottle to my lips, contemplating whether or not I wanted to know where this was going. Instead of answering, I cocked an eyebrow at him.

"I have to rescind my original statement about Conrad's new assistant. She's not just hot. She's *fucking* hot."

Toby laughed. "And the difference is…?"

Dropping my chair back onto all four legs, I stared at Leif. Okay, he'd effectively gotten my attention. I purposely ignored Toby.

"Let's just say… I'd do her."

I growled. It wasn't something I could have controlled. I didn't even realize the deep rumble had come from me until Leif's eyes widened.

"Chill, man. I'm kidding. But she is hot," Leif tacked on, smirking as he sipped his beer.

"Good for her." My tone was snide, and I realized it was too late to pretend I wasn't interested in Conrad's new assistant. If anyone saw through me, it was Leif.

"Just think, if you do her, you'll piss your father off for good," Toby blurted, evidently oblivious to the tension radiating from me.

I scowled at Toby, my anger nearly getting the best of me. As it was, I hadn't been able to stop thinking about Payton for a fucking week, but the idea of using her to piss off my old man didn't sit well with me. Not at all.

Leif laughed, tipping his own beer bottle to his lips as he studied me. "He's kidding, man."

The hell he was. "Comedy isn't your strong suit," I snapped, downing what was left of my beer.

When Toby didn't say anything more, I squeezed my beer bottle between my hands, turning my attention to Leif. He knew I wanted to know what the fuck he was talking about. Not just about Payton, but the press conference that clearly went on without me knowing. Again.

So I waited none too patiently.

"Your father was making a statement about a donation to the children's hospital. She was there with him. Not that he introduced her, but the media made a big deal out of it."

A donation. Right.

As for the media making a big deal out of Conrad's new assistant, I could understand why. I had the pleasure of meeting her, I knew what the draw was. But they made a big deal about every damn thing when it came to my father. Especially the local news. My father did a lot for the Austin area, I'd give him that. He made generous donations to various charities and he'd even sponsored a new children's hospital. All in the name of charity.

Right.

Because Conrad Trovato was so fucking charitable.

But I doubted that was the reason the media had grabbed the story. They were always looking to dig up dirt on my father. One of these days, they were going to dig just deep enough and Conrad's world was going to crumble around him.

I hoped I was there to see it.

"Have you met her yet?" Toby asked.

"Who?" I pretended not to know what they were talking about.

Thankfully our waitress arrived before either of them could continue. She delivered the wings Leif had ordered, then slid a plate of nachos in front of Toby, and I asked for another beer. After Leif had hit on her, she walked off, hopefully remembering my beer.

"I take that as a no," Leif said, staring at me.

"No," I lied.

I knew better than to tell them that yes, I'd met her. That I'd led her to believe that I was a mechanic who worked for Conrad. Or that I'd almost kissed her. They didn't need to know that.

Payton had no idea who I really was and probably never would. Just because she worked for my father, the chances of ever actually seeing her again were slim to none. Especially when it seemed Conrad was planning to stand in my way.

Not wanting to dwell on that depressing thought, I turned my attention back to the hockey game, ignoring that knowing smirk on Leif's face and the way Toby chuckled under his breath.

Assholes.

Chapter Fifteen

Payton

"Why do you insist on dragging me here every Thursday night?" I questioned Chloe as she, quite literally, dragged me toward the door of *Instant Replay*, the downtown Austin sports bar that she had turned into our Thursday night hangout.

"How many times do I have to tell you? There are hot guys who come here on Thursday night."

"I'm sure they come here every night. Hot guys, that is," I argued as I pretended to resist.

In truth, I welcomed a night of beer and hockey. After the week that I'd had, I was ready for a cold one. Or three.

Mr. Trovato had been in rare form ever since I walked through the door on Monday morning. Although I had arrived at five a.m., I found him already in his office, a cup of coffee on his desk. I think he had expected me to apologize for not being able to read his mind and show up an hour earlier than I normally did. A little rattled, I had gone on with my day, business as usual. More than once I had caught him staring at me, but it wasn't one of those creepy old guy stares. It was more like he was trying to figure me out.

If that wasn't bad enough, Conrad had taken to asking me questions. Not too personal, but definitely more so than I expected. When did I graduate? Did I enjoy school? Did my parents live close by? Did I see them often? Was I dating the guy I came to the party with? Was it serious?

Those were the questions he'd plied me with throughout the week and then some. It wasn't that I minded talking to him, but I definitely noticed a change in his demeanor. He was treating me differently. I had wondered if it had something to do with Sebastian, although, for the life of me, I couldn't figure out how. I just remembered the look on Mr. Trovato's face when I left his party with Aaron in tow. I hadn't imagined it, I knew that much.

It wasn't like I had seen Sebastian again since then. I hadn't had any reason to go to the Trovato estate and though I had dreamed about him showing up at the office, I didn't see any reason for him to do that either.

Aaron had done his best to keep me preoccupied through the week, showing up at the apartment with dinner each night, sometimes with Mark. He even stayed long enough to watch TV with Chloe and me. I knew that Chloe was curious, but I had managed to blow her off, giving her just enough details to curb her curiosity without revealing what had really happened.

Aaron, bless him, hadn't blabbed either.

Since the day after the party, we hadn't talked about Sebastian. No one. Not me. Not Aaron. Not Chloe. I think Aaron was worried about me, but I could have assured him that he had no reason to. I'd moved on. I don't know what had transpired between the two of us out on the veranda that night, but it was over and done. Thinking about Sebastian wasn't doing me any good.

I shook off the thought of him as I reached for the restaurant's front door when Chloe held it open.

Chloe and I walked inside the sports bar and one of the waitresses immediately greeted us by name, reaching for two menus before walking us to a table in the far corner. I glanced around as I walked, realizing the place was busier than usual. My gaze traveled up to one of the televisions on the wall as I walked.

Ahh… That explained it.

The Dallas Stars were playing the Nashville Predators. Always a good game to watch. I, myself, was a huge hockey fan, something I'd taken to because of my father. When I was younger, we always went to games, mostly to Dallas to see the Stars play because my dad was a diehard fan.

I bumped into Chloe when she stopped, my attention still on the television. Smiling and shrugging, I then waited for her to pick a seat — the woman was anal when it came to which chair she would take at the table. Just one of her many quirks. This time it only took her five seconds to figure it out, which was probably a record for her. I quickly hung my purse on the chair between us, choosing to sit across from her. I retrieved my cell phone before sitting down and facing my friend. Chloe was already perusing the menu, spouting off things that sounded good to her.

No way could I eat that and not gain ten pounds, but my friend, she could eat anything and not gain an ounce. Have I mentioned that I hated her for that?

"What do you think?"

"About?"

"Food, Payton. *Food.* Why do you think we came here?" Chloe asked, her eyes boring holes into me.

"I thought it was for the hot guys." I pretended to be confused.

"Well, there is that." Her gaze migrated slowly around the room.

I didn't bother to look around. I knew what I'd see. The place was a hangout for the younger crowd. Being that Austin was a college town, you didn't have to walk very far before you bumped into at least one college student. Or ten.

The waitress returned with a huge smile on her face. Chloe rattled off her order in rapid succession and I waited my turn. When she was finally finished, I smiled up at the waitress and said, "I'll have a Corona Light with lime and I'll pick off her plate."

Chloe grumbled from across the table.

"Don't worry, I'll pay for half."

"I'm not worried about that," Chloe said softly. "I'm worried about you eating half my food. I'm starving."

"You're always starving."

Chloe grinned and I knew what she was about to ask before the words even tumbled out of her mouth. The gleam in her green eyes told me everything.

"When are you gonna tell me more about that mechanic you met last week? Was he at the party?"

Yep. That was the question I was hoping to avoid.

I should have known that her silence on the subject matter had been too good to be true. As hush-hush as I'd wanted to be where Sebastian was concerned, I had been drunk when I came home on Friday night. When Aaron brought me inside, I'd resorted to thinking aloud, bitching and moaning about The Mechanic as I liked to refer to him. Chloe had been there. I think she suspected that something had happened the night of the party, but for whatever reason, she had let it go.

Obviously not completely though.

She had brought it up tonight when I got home, but because she had been ready to go out by then, I had used the fact that I needed to change as an excuse. I had again dodged her in the car, encouraging Chloe to tell me about her day and I'd hoped she wouldn't bring it back up. After all, it had been a brief lapse on my part. I should have never mentioned him to her in the first place.

But I should have known that Chloe wouldn't let it go.

"He was hot and he was a mechanic," I told her, letting her believe that the only time I'd seen him was the first day I met him. I definitely didn't want to tell her about our interaction at the party. "What more is there to say?"

"Uhh… Plenty. You can start by telling me why you don't want to talk about him," she stated, thanking the waitress when she placed the beers on the table.

Ah. So she noticed.

"Nothing to talk about. It's not like I go around talking about people's mechanics."

"Conrad Trovato really has a mechanic that works at his house? How much freaking money does this guy have?" she asked.

I could tell she was humoring me.

"Too much," I answered, going right along with her. If she could fake it, so could I.

But that statement took me back to that day. The day I met the man who had plagued my dreams before I ever met him. The same guy who had haunted my dreams for nights on end ever since. I had thought it strange, when I'd finally given it any thought at all, that Mr. Trovato had a personal mechanic that worked at his house. Even more so when I saw him at the party. He wasn't just a mechanic. I knew that much.

"What did he look like?"

"Hot." I wished she would just let it go.

As it was, I could still picture him in my head, all tall and sexy with the tats and the piercings. Then the image of him in that tux would flutter through my head. All of the tats had been covered that night, but the piercings had been visible. I even found myself daydreaming about what he looked like without his shirt on, something I hadn't had the opportunity to see.

Unfortunately.

Did he have tattoos everywhere?

"I got that part," Chloe said, interrupting my thoughts. "But what did he *look* like?"

"Tall, brown hair, brown eyes," I explained, pretending it was nothing. It was something all right because his eyes still mesmerized me, from my damn dreams. Realizing I was grinning from ear to ear, I added, "But his piercings…"

Don't ask me why I was going along with this. I was getting caught up in the moment and I didn't want to admit that talking about him made me feel better.

"In his face? Oh, God, that's hot."

Yes, it was. "Eyebrow and lip," I told her.

"What about his tongue? Was his tongue pierced?"

"How would I know?" I asked, exasperated. "I didn't get near his mouth."

Not close enough to find out if he had his tongue pierced anyway. I kept that little tidbit of info to myself.

"But you wanted to, huh?" She nudged me in the arm.

Sometimes I thought Chloe acted more like a guy than a girl. Especially when it came to talking about the opposite sex. It could have been the fact that Chloe had four brothers, all of which were just like her. Or maybe she was just like them. I didn't know.

"He was hot. Can we just leave it at that?"

"Do you think you'll go back to Mr. Trovato's house?"

"Why in the world would I do that?"

"Oh, I don't know. Maybe because you need your car serviced?"

"If that's some kind of sexual innuendo, you suck at them."

Chloe was grinning.

The two of us sat there for a moment, our eyes glued to the television. Three minutes into the third period and the Stars were up by two. I didn't really care who won. I wasn't partial to either team like my dad was. It wasn't until the waitress brought our food out that I turned my attention back to Chloe.

It was then that my night took a very interesting turn.

Chapter Sixteen

Payton

"Can I get another beer?"

The gruff voice came from behind me. At first I thought nothing of it considering we were in a sports bar full of men. A lot of men had deep, booming voices.

"Yeah, thanks," the man said.

I immediately stilled, my heart triple timing it in my chest.

That voice.

That raspy tone. It sounded familiar.

That deep baritone... it was...

No freaking way.

An elbow gently bumped my shoulder from behind. I twisted in my chair to see a man sitting directly behind me. The place was packed and we were crammed into the place like sardines, so it wasn't unusual for someone to bump me.

"Sorry about that." The brief apology caused me to turn around fully, only to come face to face with...

"Sebastian," I whispered at the same time he said, "Angel."

"I'll be damned, Trovato. Did you conjure her up from your thoughts? You're gonna have to teach me how to do that shit."

I was staring into liquid gold eyes, hardly registering what his friend was saying. But then... it clicked.

"*Trovato?*" My stomach rapidly plummeted to my feet. Sebastian *Trovato?*

Oh.

My.

God.

I had to give him credit, he looked a little embarrassed.

"You're not a mechanic," I accused, rage dripping into my blood stream. I knew my face was red, but I couldn't help it.

The devious grin he shot me didn't help.

"Oh, my God! *You're* the hot mechanic?" Chloe exclaimed, leaning over to see around me.

"Not helping, Chloe," I warned, my eyes still locked with Sebastian's.

Although I was angry, I knew the rapid beat of my heart didn't have anything to do with that. No, what had caused my heart rate to accelerate and my blood to fizz in my veins was my visceral reaction to this man. Just as he had every time I saw him — in my dream, the first time we met, at Conrad's party — Sebastian *Trovato* had captivated me.

And damn it all to hell, sitting this close to him wasn't helping.

Trovato.

Damn it.

"Why didn't you tell me who you were?" I probed, still not quite sure who he was. Conrad's nephew, maybe? With the last name of Trovato, he had to be related in some way.

"I did tell you who I was." His voice was rough, belying the amused grin on his perfect lips.

Dang it. He had a tongue ring.

Not that I was fascinated by it or anything. It's just that we were less than a foot apart and it was hard to miss when he spoke.

"You told me you were a mechanic," I stated firmly, my voice softer than before. I hated that we had an audience when I wanted to rage at him for lying to me.

"No, you *assumed* I was a mechanic."

I did not. Okay, maybe I did. Whatever.

"You didn't correct me."

"You didn't care."

No, he was right. It had never *really* mattered to me who he was. When I was in his presence, I was more worried about trying to get my libido in check.

"So did you lie to me? Are you really a mechanic?" I repeated softly, realizing he hadn't answered me moments ago.

"Mechanic." One of the guys sitting at Sebastian's table smirked, laughing as he sipped his beer.

Sebastian glanced over his shoulder at his friends before returning his gaze to mine.

"Leif, Toby, meet Angel. Angel, meet Leif and Toby."

"My name's not Angel," I snapped. I glanced over Sebastian's shoulder and forced a smile. "My name's Payton."

"Nice to meet you, Payton," the two guys said at exactly the same time, the humor dancing in their eyes was a little off-putting, mainly because I wasn't sure what the inside joke was. They were enjoying this.

Too bad I wasn't.

I met Sebastian's gaze for a long second.

"Sorry to interrupt your dinner." I broke the eye contact with Sebastian and looked past him. "Nice to meet you both."

"Feel free to interrupt anytime, Angel." Sebastian's smooth, deep voice flowed over me like silk and damn it if my body didn't light up like someone had doused me in gasoline and lit a match.

I forced my traitorous body to turn back around only to see Chloe staring at the men behind me. In truth, I'd never seen Chloe speechless. I'm not sure if I liked it or not.

"If you're gonna sit there with your mouth open, at least put something in it," I scolded Chloe, pushing the plate of nachos in her direction.

Her eyes met mine and the mischief I saw there made the hair on the back of my neck stand on end. "No. Don't you dare," I whispered, trying to keep my voice calm. "Don't you dare interfere, Chloe. Keep in mind, I need my job."

"What does he have to do with your job?" Chloe leaned in conspiratorially.

"He's obviously related to Mr. Trovato. Which means I can't get involved."

"Says who?" she inquired.

"Says me. Hurry up and eat so we can get out of here." I'd lost my appetite, and the beer suddenly tasted like dirt. I just wanted to get out of there so I didn't have to think about the fact that the hottest guy I'd ever met was sitting directly behind me, probably laughing about the fact that he'd pulled one over on me. Twice.

"Oh, God," I groaned when I remembered what I'd told Mr. Trovato upon my return to the office that day. No wonder he had looked at me like I'd lost my mind. And again at the party… When I'd been leaving, Mr. Trovato had caught me looking at Sebastian. I'd seen frustration in his eyes. Did he think…?

"What?" Chloe asked, interrupting my thoughts, her gaze roaming my face. "Spill it."

"Last week, when I went to his house to get his cell phone, I told Mr. Trovato that I hadn't seen his daughter, but I had talked to his mechanic briefly. He must think I'm a nutcase."

"Doubtful," came a voice from behind me.

I fought the urge to turn around and look at him, hoping he didn't notice the way my shoulders tensed when he spoke. His voice was a strange mixture of rough velvet and smooth silk, it pulled me in and I knew… I knew that was the last thing I needed to be worried about.

"So, how're you related to Mr. Trovato?" Chloe asked, speaking loud enough for Sebastian to hear.

I wanted to strangle her.

I felt rather than saw when Sebastian turned in his chair. He was so close, I could feel the warmth of his arm against my back although he wasn't touching me. I did my best not to move away, not wanting to let him know just how affected I was.

How freaking crazy was this? Here I was, twenty-three years old and I was acting like a teenager with a crush.

"Let's just leave it at *related*." Sebastian's grumbling voice sent chills down my spine.

"Are you done yet?" I asked Chloe, doing my best to ignore the man behind me.

Chloe's lips twitched, telling me her answer without words. She was enjoying my suffering and this was one of those times when I wished I'd brought my own car. Instead, I had let Chloe drive.

For the next fifteen or so minutes, Chloe actually paid attention to her food. Well, sort of. Her eyes kept drifting over my other shoulder and I assumed she was looking at the mammoth of a man that was sitting at Sebastian's table. Leif or Toby. I didn't know who was who.

I wasn't hungry, so I alternated between peeling the label off my beer and staring up at the television. The game was almost over and I knew when it was, the place would clear out fast.

I wanted to be gone before that happened. I wanted to be far away from here when Sebastian decided to take his leave.

The waitress returned to check on us, and to my relief, Chloe requested the bill. I dug in my purse for cash, wanting to pitch in, but Chloe put her hand on mine. "My treat. It was totally worth it."

I glared at my roommate. "I hate you," I whispered, trying to keep my expression stern.

"Of course you do."

Chapter Seventeen

Payton

By the time we were walking to Chloe's car, I was geared up to run a marathon. I just wanted to get out of there, fearful that if I didn't do something fast, I would turn right around and march back inside just to see Sebastian's handsomely smug face one last time.

I was infuriated with him. He had lied to me, convinced me that he was Mr. Trovato's mechanic.

Kind of.

The ass had told me he was a mechanic, which I guess didn't necessarily mean he worked for Conrad. But still. He had even confirmed it at the party. But what really burned me was the simple fact that his last name was Trovato, regardless of the relation to my boss, which meant he could have easily gone inside that ginormous mansion and retrieved Conrad's cell phone. But noooo… I had to go back to the office and look like an idiot when I explained that I'd had a conversation with the mechanic because Aaliyah had already left.

And then at the party… What had happened between us outside, the way my body responded to him, desperate to get closer…

But he was off limits! Off freaking limits because he was related to my boss.

Ugghh!

I wasn't sure whether I was more upset that he had lied to me or that he was off limits.

And that only pissed me off more.

"Hey, princess!" someone yelled from across the parking lot.

Don't ask me why I turned and looked. I was certainly not a princess, nor was I an angel.

It had been that damn smoky voice that had me searching the shadows for Sebastian. I caught sight of him coming toward us, while Leif and Toby (I still didn't know who was who) headed in the opposite direction.

"Hold up!" Sebastian called out as I opened the passenger side door of Chloe's car.

To my absolute horror, Sebastian walked right up to Chloe and asked to speak to her for a minute. I was seething, a red haze disrupting my vision as I watched Sebastian talk to my roommate, both of them smiling and even laughing.

What the hell? Why would he pick *her*?

I stomped my foot, unable to control myself.

Sure, Chloe was pretty. If you liked teeny tiny, green eyed, leggy brunettes. Yes, if that was your preference, she was pretty.

But I wasn't a slouch, thank you very much.

The thought had me glancing down at my outfit.

Well…

I kind of was a slouch right then.

After wearing heels for most of the day, I'd stripped right out of the skirt and, yes, another coffee-stained shirt and changed into jeans and a long sleeved, black T-shirt. It was clean. Wrinkled a little, maybe, but still clean.

I touched my hair.

It was still pulled back in a ponytail, which meant I probably looked like I was in high school. The sports bar we'd just left was perhaps the only establishment that didn't card me and that was only because I'd been coming in every week for the last few months.

But still…

"You're a doll," Sebastian told Chloe and I was ready to scream.

But then, my voice was stuck in my throat when Sebastian made his way around the car and strolled right up to me, his eyes serious. Where had all of his amusement gone?

"Let me take you home," he said softly.

"What?" I exclaimed. "No way. I don't even know you."

He merely cocked an eyebrow — the pierced one — and I got the feeling that he was used to women just giving it up to him for his crooked smile.

Not me.

No way.

"You know me well enough," he whispered.

I glanced over at Chloe and that jealousy I was feeling a moment before returned. If I didn't let him drive me home, would he offer to drive Chloe home? Would she accept?

Son of a…

"Come on, Payton. What d'ya say? We'll stop and get ice cream."

"Ice cream?" Was he serious? Ice cream. Did people really do that?

"You got something against ice cream?" Sebastian asked.

"No. I do *not* have anything against ice cream." I turned toward him, studying his face for probably longer than was appropriate. But it was the only thing I could do when I was practically sandwiched between him and the car door at my back. "What I have a problem with is leaving with you. I don't *know* you."

I knew he understood what I was telling him. He had lied to me. Whether it was by omission or not, he had let me believe something that wasn't entirely accurate.

Sebastian stared at me. He looked like he was waging a war inside his head. Did he want to tell me something?

No. He probably just wanted to blow me off, figuring I wasn't going to be a sure thing.

I was *not* going to be a sure thing.

Little did he know but I hadn't had sex in like two years, and before that, it had only been with one person. With my college boyfriend, Paul. Even then, I'm not sure that could be considered sex. Paul seemed just as inadequate as I had been for the six months that we dated.

I certainly didn't consider myself experienced in that department.

At this point, I'm not even sure that I knew how it was supposed to work. Sex, that is.

"I promise." His hand came up, the backs of his fingers brushed my arm. "I just wanna talk."

Talk.

I didn't mind talking. Maybe then he could explain just who the heck he was.

I considered it for a moment before looking back at Chloe one last time. She nodded and grinned.

"Fine," I said decisively. "We can talk."

His smile widened and I was momentarily fascinated by his lip ring.

"But only if you tell me who you are and why you lied to me."

Sebastian laughed, the sound even sexier than when he spoke. He nodded his head to Chloe. "I'll have her home in an hour. Promise."

"Okay. I'll be waiting for her," Chloe answered, looking somber for a moment.

Sebastian surprised the crap out of me when he took my hand and linked his fingers with mine. I nearly stumbled over my own feet as I stared down at our joined hands.

I hadn't held anyone's hand in… well, probably not since high school. If even then.

But the feel of Sebastian's work-roughened fingers against mine wasn't the only surprise of the night. I nearly swallowed my tongue when he stopped at the black-as-night sports car that I'd seen in the parking lot earlier.

"Is that a…?" For the life of me, I couldn't even think of the name of the car.

"A Camaro. Yeah." Sebastian chuckled as he opened the passenger side door and waited for me to climb in.

Right. A Camaro.

Oh, crap. New car smell.

After he climbed in and started the engine, I peered over at him and asked, "Is this yours?"

"Maybe." That slow smirk tilted his lips and I wanted to reach over and touch his mouth.

With mine.

Shaking off the thought, I turned and looked out the windshield. "You mentioned ice cream," I said blandly, hoping he couldn't see the lust that was likely causing smoke to seep out of my ears.

"Yes, ma'am." With that, Sebastian put the car in gear.

At that point, I held on for dear life.

Chapter Eighteen

Payton

It was a good thing Sebastian chose an ice cream shop just a few miles away. If I'd had to spend any more time in that car with him, I might have had a nervous breakdown.

I was pretty sure he didn't even know that speed limits existed.

The only positive was that he handled the car like a professional. It was both disturbing and strangely exciting. Watching him shift gears, admiring his big hands... Yeah, needless to say, I needed a cold shower more than I needed ice cream.

Luckily, Sebastian came around to open my door because, for the life of me, I couldn't figure out how to open it on my own after fumbling in the dark for a moment. From that point on, I didn't say anything until the cute girl behind the counter asked what ice cream we wanted. I was surprised that she heard me, considering she was batting her eyelashes and ogling Sebastian the entire time she was working.

Sebastian hovered close behind me while she prepared our ice cream. When she was finished, he paid and then took my hand again. I was still trying to get used to the idea of holding his hand. It was oddly settling. I felt almost... cherished. Protected.

"Let's eat outside," he said, carrying both paper bowls of ice cream.

I glanced around the inside, noticing there were three perfectly good tables available, but there was also a family sitting at one table with two little kids playing tag around a chair. Did he not like kids?

I didn't ask him because we were on the move once again and I was simply trying to remember how to walk, much less talk and walk at the same time.

"I take it you're close to Toby and Leif," I commented once we were seated at a small metal table in front of the little shop. A worn red umbrella hovering over the table flapped in the cool night breeze.

"I've known Leif since I was fourteen. Met Toby in high school."

"Do they live with you?" I didn't even know where Sebastian lived, so it was a logical question.

"Nope. At least not yet. Leif's looking for a place. We've talked about him renting a room from me."

"Do you live in a house or apartment?" I didn't mean to ply him with so many questions, but I couldn't help myself. I wanted to know everything there was to know about him. It probably would have been awkward if I'd just sat there and stared at him, too.

"House," Sebastian answered, his tone changing. I wondered if that was a sore subject. Seemed strange that he wouldn't want to talk about where he lived, but I took the hint.

"What about you? House or apartment?"

"Apartment. I live with Chloe." For some reason, I didn't want to mention that I lived with Aaron as well, which I knew wasn't completely honest. Aaron was my roommate, my best friend, but he was still a guy. Gay or not, I wasn't sure how Sebastian would take the fact that I did live with a guy so I kept my mouth shut.

A couple of family's made their way into the ice cream shop and I busied myself by watching the little kids run around in circles. Sebastian seemed to be intently studying me, and I fought the urge to squirm under his penetrating gaze.

"Why'd you let me believe you were Mr. Trovato's mechanic?" I asked bluntly, when it was clear Sebastian wasn't going to restart the conversation.

"Why'd you assume I was?"

I stared blankly at him, my spoon halfway to my mouth. "Because you were covered in grease?"

"If I'd been covered in flour would you've thought I was the cook?"

"No." My answer came just a little too quickly.

Damn it. He was right. I'd made the assumption all on my own.

"See my point yet?" Sebastian's glowing eyes locked with mine.

"Fine." I shoved the little pink plastic spoon in my mouth, accepting that he was right. The rich chocolate flavor burst on my tongue, but the only thing I could think about was how much better it would be if I could cover Sebastian in it and then lick it off.

"Quit picturing me naked," he said smoothly, arrogantly.

I narrowed my eyes at him. "In your dreams."

"That's what I'm worried about," he mumbled almost too softly to hear before spooning vanilla ice cream into his mouth.

His ice cream caught my eye and I glanced back and forth between his and mine. Chocolate and vanilla. Total opposites. Why did I have the feeling that our choice in ice cream probably wasn't the only thing different between us?

I didn't know him. Other than the way he looked, that he lived in a house not an apartment, and that he went out tonight with two guys he'd known for a long time anyway. I knew he worked for Conrad Trovato. In what capacity, I wasn't sure. I knew his last name was Trovato, which could only mean he was related to Conrad in some way. I mean seriously, Trovato wasn't a common name, so what were the odds?

I scraped my ice cream with my spoon as I met his gaze again. "Do you work for Mr. Trovato?"

"You could say that," he mumbled.

"What do you do for him?" I asked, curious.

"A little of this, a little of that."

My anger reignited and I stabbed my ice cream with my spoon. "Would you mind taking me home?" I was suddenly too frustrated to sit there with him. He'd been relatively forthcoming with my questions earlier, but they'd been significantly less personal. Seemed that when I wanted to dig deeper, he just wanted to close himself off.

I didn't want to play that game with him.

His eyes widened, the golden orbs drawing me in yet again. "Why?"

"I clearly misunderstood your reason for wanting to get ice cream. I thought we were here to talk, yet you won't give me a straight answer to any of my questions."

"Not true," he countered. "I answered you."

"Yeah," I huffed. "You told me that you live in a house. You didn't elaborate, didn't share anything more than that. And now that I want to know something more personal, you just clam up."

Sebastian didn't say anything, he turned his attention back to his ice cream, avoiding looking at me altogether.

I sighed.

"Since I'm not interested in anything else from you, aside from maybe some friendly conversation, I think it's safe to say we're done here."

I got to my feet, looking down at him.

He slowly rose from his seat and I kept my eyes locked with his until I had to look up at him.

"Look." Sebastian took my hand, watching me as though he thought I was going to run.

What was it with this guy and holding my hand? It wasn't that it didn't feel good, I was quite fond of the way he touched me, the spark that sizzled along my skin from the connection, but it disarmed me at the same time. And I had a feeling that I needed as much armor as possible when it came to Sebastian Trovato.

His thumb brushed over my knuckles a couple of times before he spoke. The sweet touch made my knees *and* my anger weaken.

"You're right," he finally said, closing his eyes briefly. "I'll take you home."

Leaving the ice cream to melt on the table, Sebastian motioned toward the car and then followed me without saying another word.

The most awkward car ride ensued, the only words spoken between us were when I had to give him directions on how to get to my apartment.

I was trying to figure out what to say, if anything, when Sebastian stopped in front of my building. I peeked over at him to find him staring down at his hand on the gear shift.

"Uhh…" I knew I at least needed to say thank you. That was the polite thing to do, right?

"Where's your boyfriend?" His words were spoken so softly, they were hard to make out.

"What?" I was confused.

He looked up, meeting my gaze in the darkness. "The guy you were with at the party. Your boyfriend. Why aren't you with him tonight?"

127

Oh, crap. I'd let him believe that Aaron was my boyfriend.

I looked away quickly, choosing to stare out the windshield while I tried to gather my thoughts.

"He's not your boyfriend, is he?" Sebastian questioned.

"No," I admitted, hating the fact that he'd caught me in a lie. Aaron had been my excuse, the only logical excuse I had to stay far, far away from Sebastian.

"Then who is he?"

I closed my eyes, trying to come up with an answer that wouldn't make me sound like I had lied to him or led him to believe something that wasn't true. The way he had done to me.

Before I could get the words out, Sebastian surprised me by reaching over and sliding his hand behind my neck, pulling me to him. One minute he was sitting still, the next he was pulling me toward him, his mouth meeting mine. He wasn't rough, but he wasn't gentle either. And when our lips touched, all of my air escaped in a pathetic little sigh.

His tongue slid over my bottom lip before coaxing its way into my mouth. I reached for him, unable to resist the opportunity to touch him. His shoulders were hard, the muscles tense beneath the navy T-shirt he wore. The short hair on the back of his head sensually scraped against my palm as my tongue slid against his. To my utter embarrassment, I moaned. And that only spurred Sebastian on. He pulled me closer, our lips crushed together as he devoured me. That was the only description for what was happening between us.

And holy crap! It was a good thing I was sitting down because my legs had turned to jelly, my entire body quaking from the intensity of his kiss.

I slid my hands higher, pulling his hair gently, sinking my fingers into the longer locks on the top. Oh, God. What was I doing?

I knew absolutely nothing about this man other than he was a shitty conversationalist and the world's greatest kisser and though my brain was screaming for me to pull away, to jump out of the car and run far and fast, I couldn't do it. I was scared if he kept kissing me, I was going to figure out a way to climb his body and that would be a devastation that I'd never survive.

But then he was pulling away, nibbling at my lips briefly before his eyes met mine. His hand was still cupping my nape, his thumb rasping over my cheek. We were both breathless, and I still wasn't trying to get away from him.

"So, no boyfriend?"

I shook my head.

"Then we're even."

I knew what he was referring to. He had led me to believe he was Conrad's mechanic, and I had led him to believe Aaron was my boyfriend. So, yes, we were even.

"Let me see you again, Angel," Sebastian whispered, resting his forehead against mine. "I…" He paused, his eyes still peering into mine. "I just need to see you again."

"Why?" I asked, wanting to know.

It was clear he didn't want to tell me anything about himself, and I'd been honest when I said that was what I wanted from him. I was quite capable of controlling my own hormones, although you might not be able to tell it by the way I'd kissed him as though my life depended on it.

"I can't explain it."

I couldn't either. And none of it made sense.

I'd met guys like Sebastian. They were the bad boys that good girls like me stayed away from, the ones that were looking for fast and dirty sex — something I was pretty sure I couldn't even offer, thank you very much.

With every intention of telling him that we'd be better off just moving along, I was shocked to the roots of my hair when I whispered, "Why don't I give you my phone number and we'll see how it goes?"

Sebastian pulled away and I immediately missed the warmth of his hand on my neck. "Let me see your phone," he stated gently, his eyes never leaving mine.

I grabbed my phone from my purse and handed it to him as though there wasn't anything weird about giving it to a complete stranger.

He's not too much of a stranger, you know what his lips feel like.

I ignored that little voice in my head while I watched him dial a number. A second later, his cell phone rang. He hung up and then did the opposite, calling my phone from his number.

"Done."

Yes, I guess we were. "Okay, then." I twisted in my seat, ready to reach for the door handle.

Once again, Sebastian caught me off guard when he reached for me. This time his lips brushed mine ever so gently and I breathed him in. He smelled good. Something spicy and rich and I wanted to inhale him until the scent was embedded in my brain.

"I need to see you again," he whispered against my lips, and this time, I heard the desperation in his tone. Or was that just lust?

It was strange. It didn't sound like he was trying to push me to invite him in, but that he truly wanted to see me again in the future. And as upset as I was at him for duping me earlier in the day, I couldn't lie and say that I didn't want the same thing.

Rather than drag it out any longer, I leaned in and pressed my mouth to his, feeling the metal of his lip ring against my bottom lip. Unable to resist, I slid my tongue over the cool metal, but I didn't linger past that. I nodded my head and then reached for the door handle, finding it instantly although I hadn't even seen it earlier.

Without another word, I climbed out and closed the door, glancing back one more time as I made my way up the stairs. Sebastian's car remained in the parking lot until I entered my apartment.

Once inside, I quickly closed and locked the door behind me. As I listened until the throaty rumble of the car's engine disappeared into the night, I closed my eyes and leaned against the front door, wondering just what I was supposed to do now.

Chapter Nineteen

Payton

By noon the following day, I was counting down the seconds until I could go home. Conrad had taken the day off, but I still had to remain in the office to field his phone calls and work on the logistics for an upcoming trip he was taking to Las Vegas. Apparently the SEMA show was as big a deal for Trovato, Inc. as it was for my father and his little body shop. Then again, they were both in the automotive industry, so it made sense. With the trip coming up next week, I had to finalize the details. Thankfully, Jasmine had scheduled everything months ago, so I was just confirming that it was all still in order.

I was pretty sure the universe was out to get me because, from the time I arrived at eight, coming in later because Mr. Trovato wasn't going to be in the office, the phone rang all of seven times. Two of those had been solicitors that I had politely asked not to call back. I had learned already that when Mr. Trovato was out of the office, no one generally came to see him, which was no different today. I was sitting on the second floor by myself, willing the phone to ring so I'd at least have someone to talk to for a few minutes.

The rest of the time I was thinking about Sebastian and the kiss we'd shared the night before. I couldn't stop replaying his words over and over in my head. *I need to see you again.* It hadn't slipped past me that he'd used the word "need" rather than "want." And when he said it, that was exactly how it made me feel. As though it was critical that we didn't let this end before it ever got started.

The universe must have heard me moaning and groaning because the phone on my desk rang. I eagerly reached for it, answering with "Trovato, Inc. Conrad Trovato's office. How may I help you?"

"Payton."

I instantly sat up straight when I heard my boss's voice on the phone. I hadn't expected him to call, and a million things ran through my mind. Was he upset? Did I do something wrong? Was he going to fire me on the phone?

Don't ask me why I got so antsy, I just did.

"Yes, sir?" I replied, holding my breath.

"You're working on the trip to Vegas next week, right?"

"Yes, sir."

"Good. I need you to plan to go with me."

Oh, no. Please no. I did not want to travel. It just wasn't my thing.

Not that I could tell Conrad that. My job was to assist him and, technically, if he needed me to go along on a business trip with him, I wasn't supposed to argue. "Okay," I answered hesitantly.

"My wife and daughter will be coming along. Book yourself a hotel room. Make sure you're in the same hotel that we are."

"Yes, sir." It seemed those were the only two words that still existed in my vocabulary.

"Thanks, Payton. I'll see you Monday morning."

"Yes, sir."

There was a click, signaling that Conrad had hung up, so I dropped the receiver in the cradle and stared at my computer screen.

Las Vegas.

I'd never been to Las Vegas.

I wasn't sure I wanted to go to Las Vegas.

Knowing that fretting about it wasn't going to get me anywhere, I typed in the web address for the hotel where Mr. Trovato was staying. After attempting to locate a room using their online tool, I came up empty. No rooms were available for that time frame. I figured it had to do with the show.

Maybe that was how I could get out of it. If they didn't have a room, I wouldn't have to go.

Knowing that Conrad would expect me to call them directly, I grabbed the receiver and dialed the number that Jasmine had noted with the reservation.

Twenty minutes later I wasn't feeling any better. The kind woman on the other end of the phone had only been too happy to help me, instantly getting an additional room for Mr. Trovato. Apparently he was a VIP and the lady had been quite enamored when I mentioned his name.

Crap.

So much for lucking out on that one.

Once that was done, I took care of the flight, encountering another very helpful employee at the airline who ensured me they had an additional seat in first class, on the same flight Mr. Trovato and his family would be on.

Great.

I had just finished taking care of everything, printing out my itinerary for the trip and urging my stomach to stop churning. I knew that being an administrative assistant wasn't just going to consist of me sitting in the office and answering Conrad's phones, but I had truly hoped that I wouldn't have to travel with the man. Sure, it helped that Aaliyah was going. I liked her. I figured we'd get along well, but still.

My cell phone chirped from inside my desk drawer while I was still staring blankly at the computer screen.

Without a second of hesitation, I snatched it, hitting the button to bring the screen to life. The words I saw there made all of my previous worries disappear instantly.

Dinner with me tonight.

That's all the text said, but I knew who the number belonged to because last night, after I'd managed to get my heart rate back under control, I had added Sebastian's number to my contact list, not wanting to accidentally delete it.

Who is this?

I sent a text back, smiling as I did.

Your mechanic

Now, if I said my heart didn't skip a beat, I'd be lying.

Mine. He was *mine?*

My fingers were shaking, my nerves in an uproar as I typed a message back.

I'm not sure I need my car serviced at the moment, but thank you anyway.

The response didn't come quickly and I was starting to think Sebastian had taken me seriously. I was still staring at my phone a minute later when the next message finally came in.

That's good cuz I wanted to take you to dinner, not service your… um… car

I felt the heat rise to my face. He'd effectively embarrassed me and I was grateful that he couldn't see me right then. Caving, I shot a quick message back. *When?*

"Right now."

I fell out of my chair.

Yep, without an ounce of grace, I fell right out. Of. My. Chair.

I would have been embarrassed, except the shock to my heart was so powerful, I was gasping for breath and holding my hand against my chest, trying to keep the damn organ from jumping up through my throat.

"You scared me," I declared, pushing to my feet before Sebastian could help me. He was faster than I was, his strong hands gripping my arms when I stood. "How'd you get up here?" I peeked around him, fully expecting Ron to come up the stairs ready to shoot to kill.

"I'm persuasive like that," Sebastian answered. "Are you okay?"

135

Okay? Was I okay? No, I was not. I was embarrassed and happy to see him all at the same time. "I'm fine. Just call me grace," I mumbled, looking down at the floor.

The silence was stifling until Sebastian used his finger to tip my chin up, forcing me to look at him. "Are you ready?"

No, I wasn't sure I'd ever be ready for anything this man had to offer me.

I didn't tell him that though. I simply nodded before I could think better of it.

It took me a minute to shut down my laptop and place it in the bag, but once I did, Sebastian retrieved it from my desk and put it on his arm. His big, bulging, muscular arm. The one decorated with tattoos.

I still wanted to know how he'd slipped past the security guard.

Maybe it was his last name.

"Time's wasting." His silky voice sent a shiver racing through me.

I nodded, not sure what else to do. Tossing my cell phone in my purse, I hauled it onto my shoulder and glanced back at my desk one last time.

It was only four, and I had no idea whether or not Mr. Trovato would be angry that I left early, but my boredom was going to have me running out the door screaming if I didn't go now anyway.

There was no hand holding as I followed Sebastian out of the building. I looked around to see if I could find the Camaro he'd been driving the day before. I saw a multitude of cars, but none of them was his sleek black car.

"Where'd you park?" he asked as he stepped off the curb in front of the building.

"Me?" Wow, that sounded stupid. "I thought you were taking *me* out."

"I am."

"Then why are we taking my car?"

"Who said we were?"

136

I glared at Sebastian. The man was infuriating and way too cryptic.

That's when he took my hand and his simple touch jolted me instantly. He could have said we were walking and I wouldn't have argued with him at that point.

Chapter Twenty

Sebastian

I knew I was taking a chance when I showed up at my father's office to see Payton unannounced. After last night, anything I did where Payton was concerned was a risk, but I couldn't help myself. The minute I learned that Conrad and his wife had gone out of town, I knew what I had to do.

Waiting until four o'clock had been the kicker. I'd spent the day screwing with my truck until finally I got the damn thing running the way it should. How I managed that, I still had no idea. My thoughts had been on Payton since I pulled out of her apartment complex the night before. Even then, I knew that staying away from her was going to be impossible, but I hadn't wanted to look too desperate.

Whatever it was about her, I needed more. And need was a strong word, but I was drawn to her in a way I'd never been drawn to anyone the way I was to Payton, let alone a woman. Since I didn't know her all that well, I wasn't quite sure what the allure was, but I'd be damned if I wasn't going to try and find out.

When we reached her Mustang, I waited for her to unlock the door. I slipped her computer bag inside and then put my hands on her hips before she could disappear inside the car, too. "What are you hungry for?" I asked, trying to keep from touching her too much.

I didn't know Payton well enough to be touching her period, but I felt a connection to her. Maybe it sounded fucked up, but it was as though she and I had been destined to meet. Despite my ability to frustrate her to no end with my lack of conversational skills, I wanted her to like me. I wanted her to want me.

I wanted her to *need* me.

After spending just a few minutes in her presence, the woman unhinged me. Even as fucked up as I was, it didn't matter. I swore to do whatever it took to make her want me.

"Pizza," she said quickly, her eyes roaming my face.

I smiled down at her, admiring the intriguing color of her eyes. Last night I noticed they were an unusual shade of yellow-green. Today they were just green. It probably had a lot to do with the emerald green sweater she wore, the one that outlined every luscious curve.

Pulling my eyes away from said curves, I met her gaze. "Pizza?" I was a little surprised by her selection.

"You got something against pizza?" She used the same phrase I'd used on her the night before, her smile radiant as she rested her palms on my chest. Seeing her look so happy made me want to do whatever was necessary to ensure that smile stayed in place.

"Pizza works." Hell, I'd eat dirt if it meant I got to have dinner with her. "I'll meet you at your apartment."

"Do I have time to change?"

"If you want. I happen to think you look good enough to eat," I told her, glancing back down at her breasts before slowly sliding my gaze up to hers once again.

The pink that infused her cheeks made me feel invincible, like I could conquer the world. The idea of her feeling a little off-kilter was empowering, something I hadn't felt before.

"Okay." Her eyes darted away from mine quickly. "But you'll have to let me go if you expect me to drive home."

I didn't want to let her go, I wanted to feel the warmth of her skin beneath my palms, but I knew she was right. I nodded, releasing my grip on her hips and taking a step back. Her hands fell from my chest and I wanted to grab hold of them and plant them there again just so she didn't stop touching me.

Moving out of the way, I stood by patiently until she climbed into her car and closed the door. Resting my hand on the roof, I waited until she started the engine before backing up. And it wasn't until her car pulled out of the parking lot that I started walking to my truck.

I glanced up at the building, wondering just what my father was going to say when he found out I was dating his assistant. He had already warned me to stay away from her. Not that I ever intended to listen.

I had a sneaking suspicion that I was pushing too hard this time. But I didn't give a shit.

Conrad and I didn't see eye to eye on many things. He hated my piercings, cringed when he caught a glimpse of my tattoos, and he detested my choice in music. But Conrad Trovato loved money more than he loved anything, so he managed to overlook much of what I did, only because I was the one who'd put his fucking company on the map.

Performance engines were my specialty. I had taken a personal interest in Trovato, Inc. as soon as I found out that my father owned it. I made it my mission to show him that he wasn't all that. I'd proven myself by doing what his best engineers couldn't do. And I didn't have to sit behind a desk every day to do it. That was the best part.

I pulled out onto the street when there was a break in traffic and I slammed my foot on the gas, the truck took off, the engine growling. I smiled to myself at the thought of all those people in that building who still had no idea who I was. There were only a handful of people who knew that I was Conrad Trovato's son. A very limited few. And I wouldn't be surprised if those people had been threatened within an inch of their lives if they disclosed what they knew.

I certainly wasn't going to be the one to break the news to anyone.

Well, except for Payton.

I knew I had to tell her. If I expected this to go anywhere at all, I had to tell her all about myself.

I only hoped she didn't freak. That was one of the reasons I was trying to hold off until I could make an impression on her… a good impression. I wanted her to think about me the way I had thought about her for the last week. And then I'd tell her all of the tragic details of my life.

Pulling up in front of her apartment building, I didn't bother pulling into a parking space. I probably should have done the gentlemanly thing and gone to her door, but I couldn't. I feared that if she let me in, ordering pizza would be the extent of dinner because if we had just a little privacy, I wasn't going to be able to keep my hands off her.

And that wasn't going to go over well with Payton. Not on a first date, for sure.

My attention was drawn to the stairs when I noticed her coming toward me. She'd changed into a pair of faded jeans and a T-shirt, just a little more casual than what she'd worn to work.

I decided right then and there that those jeans were now my favorite. Even from this distance, I could see that there was a hole in the thigh and I got a glimpse of golden skin beneath. I would have preferred she put on a skirt so I could get an eyeful of her incredible legs, but this would work, too.

"Nice truck," she complimented when she climbed in. "What year is it?"

"'63."

"Did you restore it yourself?"

"I did."

Just like the Camaro, I'd dumped a lot of money into the truck. New interior, new cherry-red paint job. It cost a pretty penny. But what was under the hood said it all.

"Nice job," she said approvingly.

"Thanks. So pizza, huh?"

After searching the seat around her, Payton peered up at me from the other side of the cab, her eyebrows raised in question.

"What?"

"Seatbelts?"

I chuckled. "Sorry, this one didn't come with seatbelts. But you don't need 'em if you come sit by me."

"I don't need one? I do remember how you drove last night, you know."

"I'd been showing off then," I lied. I hadn't been showing off. That was how I drove. Speed was the name of the game. I was an adrenaline junkie, there was no doubt about it, which was why the license plate on the Camaro read *BLUR* and the main reason I had roll bars installed in it. The truck, however, did not have roll bars. "I'll be more careful this time."

I patted the seat and watched her.

I noticed the instant she decided to give in. She scooted toward me and I kept my hand on the shifter on the steering column. Three on the tree in the middle of downtown Austin meant my hand would be otherwise occupied, unfortunately, but having her beside me was enough.

Thirty minutes later, I pulled into a small pizza place downtown. Traffic was a bitch, especially since they were preparing to close Sixth Street off to through traffic for the night, but I managed to make my way to a parking garage close by.

"You don't mind walking, do you?" I asked, after we had parked.

"If I said I did?" Payton retorted, a glowing grin on her face.

I couldn't resist the urge to kiss her. It was overwhelming with its intensity so I leaned over and pressed my mouth to hers. The soft purr that escaped her had my body hardening instantly.

Shit.

Starting the night off with a hard-on wasn't going to go over well, but that's just what happened. My body responded to her, the taste of her lips, the light floral fragrance of her hair… I couldn't get enough.

Pulling back before I took things too far, I placed both hands on the steering wheel and stared out the windshield, taking deep breaths.

"You okay?" I could hear the amusement in her tone.

"Never better," I whispered, rather impressed that my voice worked at all. Inhaling sharply, I gripped the door handle before glancing over at her. "Come on. Let's eat."

The walk to the pizza joint took us fifteen minutes, but Payton spent most of the time talking about the bars, tattoo parlors, and stores that lined the main drag. I'd taken her hand as soon as she climbed out of the truck and hadn't let go. I didn't intend to let go. Not until I needed to use that hand to eat, and I was even debating that.

When we reached the pizza place, I pulled open the door and a bell rang overhead, announcing our presence. The short, heavy set man with thick black hair and a wide grin glanced up and smiled from behind the register.

"Trovato!" he greeted, making his way out from behind the register. "How the hell ya been?"

Payton was staring at me like I had two heads coming off my shoulders, but I just clutched her hand as Rocco approached. I didn't let her go even when Rocco insisted on throwing his burly arms around me and squeezing, jarring my teeth with numerous slaps on my back.

"Rocco, this is Payton. Payton, this is Rocco. He's an old friend."

Payton smiled and held out her hand, but just as I expected, Rocco reached for her, thankfully not slapping her on the back but hugging her hard enough for her to let out a startled squeak.

"Be easy, Rocco," I warned playfully.

"No, it's fine," Payton said, sounding a little breathless.

"What can I get you kids?" Rocco asked as he turned back toward the counter.

We fell into step behind him and I looked at Payton for suggestions.

"Pepperoni."

"My kinda girl," I teased, turning my attention to Rocco.

A few minutes later we were seated at one of the booths with the red and white checkered table cloths. Rocco brought two beers in clear plastic cups before disappearing into the back.

The restaurant was surprisingly empty, but I knew that would change. It was Friday night and the college campus wasn't far. Pretty soon, the place would be full of people laughing and joking, grabbing a bite to eat before a night on the town.

"How do you know him?" Payton asked when we were alone.

"He was friends with my mom," I told her, realizing instantly what I'd just said.

"*Was?*"

I stared at Payton for a moment. Honest to God, I wanted to tell this girl anything she wanted to know, but I didn't want to start the date off like that. But I couldn't leave her hanging. "How about this," I started, reaching for her hand quickly. I brushed my thumb over her knuckles. "I'll tell you all the personal details you want to know, but… Wait, let me finish."

Payton huffed, making me smile.

"I'll bare my soul to you, but let's wait until the second date. Tonight's about having fun. Deal?"

Payton didn't look at all good with the suggestion, but she finally agreed. "Fine." Her frown turned into a mischievous grin and I knew I wasn't going to like what came next. "Under one condition."

"Hit me."

"No more kissing until you answer my questions."

The woman drove a hard bargain, I'd give her that. "No promises, Angel," I told her, keeping my voice low. "As much as I'd like to say I was good with that, I'd be lying through my teeth."

Payton looked a little shocked by my honesty. She was also momentarily speechless, but just as I expected, that didn't last long.

"So what's a safe subject?" she asked just as Rocco was bringing the pizza out to the table. He handed us paper plates and napkins before leaving us alone again.

"You," I suggested. "Tell me about you."

"What do you want to know?" she asked, reaching for a slice of pizza.

I loved the fact that she didn't pretend to be a bird, didn't act as though one bite of pizza would require her to spend two months at the gym. No, not Payton. She grabbed a slice and took a bite before I could even come up with a question.

"What are you smiling at?" Payton was studying me as she reached for a napkin and then wiped the sauce from her lips.

"You," I admitted truthfully.

"Well, quit."

Not a chance in hell. There hadn't been a damn thing in my life to smile at for as long as I could remember, but now, with Payton, I wasn't sure I would ever stop smiling.

"Are you from Austin?" I asked after snatching a slice of pizza.

"Yep. Born and raised," she admitted. "My parents are from here, too."

"They still married?"

"Yeah. My dad owns a body shop and my mother's a CPA."

"Brothers or sisters?" I asked between bites.

"Nope. Only child."

"Did your dad restore your Mustang?"

"He helped. He owns a body shop, so it was a project they all undertook for a while. It was a gift for my eighteenth birthday."

"Not a fan of the Mustang?"

"It's fine. I just wish it was a little more… modern."

"But it's a classic."

"That it is. And by classic, I think you mean old."

"Not quite what I meant, but okay, I get your point." Laughing, I consumed my pizza, watching Payton do the same. Was it strange that I found the way she ate pizza incredibly sexy?

While Payton stopped at one slice, I had four. By the time we finished, the place was filled to capacity. I had to wrap my arm around her — certainly not a hardship — just so we could make it to the door.

Once outside, the scent of gasoline and fall assaulted me.

"Where to now?" Payton asked as we strolled down Sixth Street once again.

"It's your night. You tell me."

"Why is it my night?" She peered up at me as she spoke.

I just wanted to push her against the building and ravage her mouth until neither of us knew what day it was.

But I didn't.

I was trying to control myself. That's what you did on a first date, right? Especially if you wanted the first date to lead to another. And then another.

"Because it is," I told her. "Want to stop in one of the bars?"

"Sure. You pick though. I'm not good at that."

"Picking bars?"

"Picking anything." Payton's smile was beautiful. So damn beautiful.

As we walked down the street, I pointed to one of the tattoo shops. "That's where I got most of my work done."

"Really?" Payton stopped suddenly, looking up at me. "How much art do you have?"

"Not much more than what you see," I told her. My arms and my shoulders were the main areas I'd focused on. I had a cross on my back, between my shoulder blades.

"Do they have meaning behind them?" she asked, still not moving.

"Some do. Some don't. There for a while, I just did it to piss off…" I stopped myself immediately, realizing that I was headed down a conversational dead end.

"Off limits tonight, huh?" She obviously understood why I stopped.

"Just tonight," I explained, squeezing her hand.

"Okay." Payton's eyes slid down to my mouth.

I could feel the heat in her gaze and I desperately wanted to kiss her. It didn't matter that we were standing in the middle of a crowded sidewalk on one of the busiest streets in downtown Austin for a Friday night. I couldn't promise her that I wouldn't kiss her for the rest of the night, but I did remember her stipulation. For now, I was going to do my damnedest to give her what she asked for.

"Come on. Let's see how much trouble we can get in." I forced a smile, my brain working overtime on how I was supposed to not kiss her. The temptation was just too great.

After all, the night was still young.

Chapter Twenty-One

Payton

The following morning, I found myself lying in my bed, unable to get up.

Although it was November, and the temperature at night hovered somewhere in the low fifties, it still managed to get cold in the apartment thanks to the crappy insulation. No one seemed to have a problem with the colder temperatures except me. Chloe liked the cold and Aaron hadn't been home enough for it to matter to him. And since Chloe was anal when it came to controlling the thermostat, the heater obviously wasn't on, which was why I was snuggled beneath the down comforter on my bed, staring around my room. I was freezing.

Chloe was the reason I was awake. She was the reason I was usually up early every Saturday morning, in fact. The woman was up with the sun, another one of her many quirks. And on Saturday mornings, she always got up and made blueberry pancakes while singing in the kitchen.

It sounded worse than it was.

The woman could sing. I mean she could belt out a tune like nobody's business. It was incredible and there were certainly worse ways to wake up.

But now that my eyes were open, the sun peeking in through the curtains on my window, I thought back to last night.

First date.

Yep, that had been a first date to top all first dates.

After Sebastian and I had left the pizza place, we stopped to watch a guy paint mind-blowing pictures using just spray paint and little cardboard cutouts. I hadn't been in any hurry to move on, especially when Sebastian wrapped his arms around me, allowing me to lean against his chest. We probably stood there for a solid half hour and during that time, the guy with the spray paint completed three pictures. They were incredible.

By two o'clock, Sebastian and I had decided to call it a night. We'd spent several hours people watching, laughing and joking about random things and keeping our conversation light and impersonal.

At first, I'd been disappointed that Sebastian didn't want to open up to me, but when I recognized the storm clouds in his brilliant gold gaze, I knew whatever he was holding back was hard for him. That didn't mean I didn't want to know, but I also didn't want for our date to go to crap right off. So, we'd had a couple of beers early on at one of the popular bars on Sixth Street and then closed the place down at two. We'd stopped drinking early, so it hadn't been the alcohol talking when I had wanted to take him back to my apartment and ravish him until dawn.

Just like the personal conversation, that hadn't happened either, and now I was wondering when I'd get to see him again.

There was a light tap on my bedroom door before it flew open and in strolled Chloe. She was wearing an oversized T-shirt that read "My imaginary friend thinks you have serious mental problems." That was one of her favorites, although she had a drawer full of different ones.

"Mornin' sunshine!" Chloe exclaimed moments before she flung herself onto my bed and cuddled up beside me. "Whatcha doin'?"

"Just laying here," I told her, pulling the blanket up to my nose. I don't know how the girl could stand it to be so cold in the apartment, but she was the culprit who continued to turn down the temperature until ice was practically forming on the air vents. I would admit that it probably wasn't quite cool enough outside to turn on the heater, but I was pretty sure we could have gone without the air conditioner for a couple of weeks.

"How'd your date go?" she asked, flopping onto her back and staring at the ceiling along with me.

"Amazing," I told her, unable to stop the grin from forming on my face.

"Yeah?" Chloe turned her head to the side and looked at me. "So, the mechanic can fix more than just cars, can he?"

"Shut up," I scolded her, laughing. "It was nice."

"Nice. I'm sure that sexy bad boy would love to know you called him nice."

"I didn't call him nice. I said the date was nice."

"I'm sure that's what he was going for," Chloe said with a laugh. "What time did you get home?"

"It was after two. Where were you anyway?" I turned my head to look at her.

Chloe wasn't home when I arrived, so I hadn't had anyone to share the details of my date with. Which was probably a good thing because, at the time, I'd been floating on a cloud and I would have sounded pathetic.

"Out."

"That's it. That's all you're gonna tell me?" I asked, turning my head and looking at the ceiling again.

"Yup!" she squealed and jumped to her feet. "Breakfast's ready. Come eat with me."

The only reason I agreed was because my stomach grumbled loudly, reminding me that I'd only had one slice of pizza for dinner last night and that had been early. If I had been out with Chloe or Aaron, I would have had at least two, but with Sebastian, I didn't want to look like a pig so I'd cut myself off.

The scent of sweet blueberries drifted from the kitchen, seemingly calling out to my stomach. Snatching my white, fluffy robe from the small chair beside my bed, I wrapped it around myself and followed Chloe to the kitchen.

I nearly tripped over my own two feet when I stepped into the small breakfast area.

There, sitting in one of the kitchen chairs was…

"Payton, you remember Toby."

"I… uh…" Yeah, I remembered him. Although I hadn't been positive what his name was, but I certainly remembered him.

I patted my hair, wondering just how bad I looked and then decided to slip into the bathroom. Although, *run to the bathroom* was a more apt description.

Sebastian's friend Toby was in our kitchen.

Our kitchen.

Toby.

And Chloe was still in her pajamas.

I stared at myself in the mirror above the sink, trying to remember what Toby had been wearing. Jeans and a T-shirt, maybe? Did he have on shoes? The powers of deductive reasoning were telling me that Toby had spent the night. But I was hoping that I was missing something.

Why didn't Chloe mention this to me before? Why would she let me stumble out of my bedroom looking like death warmed over just to find a strange man in my kitchen?

After brushing my teeth, I splashed cold water on my face and massaged the skin beneath my eyes, willing myself to look more awake. I took a brush to my hair but then decided to pull it back in a ponytail. Without makeup, I really did look like a teenager, but at the moment, it beat the alternative: looking like a zombie apocalypse had started and they'd taken me first.

Shit.

A gentle knock on the door had me spinning around and clutching my hand to my chest.

"You okay in there?" Chloe called from the other side of the door.

No. I wasn't. But that's not what I said. "Yep. Be out in a sec." I hoped my voice sounded more chipper than I felt.

"You can do this," I told the woman in the mirror. "Just walk out there and have a civil conversation with Sebastian's friend. It doesn't matter why he's here. It doesn't even matter that he might've stayed the night."

Like hell.

Another splash of cold water on my face and I was scrubbing it off with a hand towel before tightening the belt on my robe and reaching for the door knob.

Part of me expected to see Chloe standing in the hallway, ready to tell me just what the hell was going on, but the only thing that met me was the lingering scent of pancakes and syrup.

Taking a deep breath, I pasted a smile on my face and walked into the living room.

"Oh, my God!" I squealed like an idiot, spun on my heel and darted into my bedroom before slamming the door behind me.

Sebastian was in my kitchen.

Oh crap. Oh crap. Oh crap.

I buried my face in my hands and started laughing uncontrollably.

Chapter Twenty-Two

Payton

I had no idea how long I stood there like that, but then there was a knock on my door. "Come in." I could hardly speak through my laughter, but I figured Chloe was back to check on me so I forced the words out.

"Hey."

I was pretty sure I had a minor heart attack. Grateful that my bed was close by, I dropped to my butt and stared at the sexy man standing in my bedroom doorway.

"You okay?" he asked, that mischievous gleam in his eyes disarming me.

"Nope. Not okay," I mumbled loudly. "Not sure I'll be okay ever again."

That only seemed to intensify his amusement, and Sebastian moved into the room and closed the door behind him.

Shit.

Not good.

"What…" I closed my mouth, cleared my throat and tried again. "What…?" *are you doing here?* I couldn't seem to get the last part of the sentence out of my mouth, but I knew I was gaping at Sebastian.

"Cat got your tongue, Angel?" Sebastian stalked closer to me.

That was the only way to explain the predatory gleam in his beautiful eyes. I felt like a mouse who'd been cornered by a cat, and I didn't know quite what to do about it.

The next thing I knew, I was on my back with my feet resting on the floor, and Sebastian was above me. His hands were planted firmly on the bed as he held himself up. I was in desperate need of air because being this close to him was...

"Good morning," he whispered in that raspy tone that I'd come to want more of.

I was suddenly grateful that I had brushed my teeth.

"Morning." Oh, Lord. Was that my voice? Did I just croak?

The smirk that tilted the corner of Sebastian's mouth sent my hormones into overdrive. I could feel the warmth of his body through my robe although he wasn't touching me.

I cleared my throat, intent on not looking like a love-struck fool as I lay beneath him, staring up at his handsome face. "What are you doing here?"

"Toby mentioned breakfast."

"Why is Toby here?" I felt a little better now that I'd found my voice again. The fact that Sebastian was still hovering above me was doing strange things to my insides, but at least I sounded like I was unaffected.

Maybe.

"Chloe invited him."

"So he didn't stay the night?" I attempted to sit up only to find that Sebastian wasn't going to move.

"Not my business," Sebastian murmured, his eyes drifting down to my mouth.

No, it wasn't. Nor was it my business, but I had to admit, I wasn't used to waking up to find strange men in our apartment. I'd lived with Chloe for the last year after I'd decided that in order to save money, I needed to take on an additional roommate. Aaron and I had been in a two bedroom apartment until I met Chloe when I decided to try a new hair stylist closer to where we'd moved. From the moment we started talking, we'd been instant friends and a few short months later, Aaron and I moved to a three bedroom apartment following the logic that with three people splitting the rent we'd save more money.

It had worked, and until now, especially with Aaron always gone, things had been rather boring at home.

Finding strange men in my kitchen first thing in the morning took boring and shattered it into a million pieces.

"What are you thinking about?"

Sebastian's question pulled me from my thoughts. "Nothing. What are *you* thinking about?" I realized he was still looking at my mouth.

"Kissing you. It's the only thing I *can* think about."

Okay, so that one sentence sent a torrent of tingles through my insides. I was tempted to rub up against him like a cat, wanting to press my body to his, to feel every hard plane of his body against me. Thankfully my legs were shut, but I couldn't move because Sebastian was practically straddling me, his feet still planted firmly on the floor, legs spread wide, his knees trapping my thighs between them.

"Well, you know the rules," I whispered, wishing the rules would take a flying leap right out the window. I wanted him to kiss me. I'd wanted that since I made the stupid rule in the first place.

Sebastian had thrown me for a loop last night. After we had left the pizza place, aside from holding my hand and putting his arms around me while we'd watched the painter, we hadn't touched at all. No kissing, no making out in the parking lot. Nothing.

And even when he had walked me to my door at two-thirty in the morning, he didn't even offer a good night kiss. It had left me desperately wanting him.

I was pretty sure that was his plan.

"I do know the rules," he said softly. "But you know what I think about rules?"

"Hmm?" I asked, unable to tear my gaze from his lips. When he talked, I could see the silver barbell through his tongue.

Sebastian didn't answer my question with words. He simply leaned down and pressed his lips to mine.

It was like an explosion occurred inside me. Unable to resist, I threw my arms around his neck and kissed him back. I was the aggressor, forcing my tongue into his mouth until we were crushed together. The growl that erupted from him made my body ignite and I feared that I was going to go up in a puff of smoke any minute now.

"Angel," he growled against my lips, his hand sliding behind my head.

The next thing I knew, Sebastian was flat on the bed and I was lying on top of him, straddling his hips. I could feel his erection pressing against me and holy smokes, I wanted more of him.

But he didn't touch me and I didn't touch him, other than where our bodies were resting against one another. His tongue dueled with mine and his hands were cupping my head, but he wasn't trying to cop a feel.

God, I wanted him to cop a feel.

Shit.

Now I was acting like a horny teenager.

Someone pounded on the door and I drew my mouth from Sebastian's, staring down at him.

"Come on, kids. Time to eat," Toby called through the door.

I giggled when Sebastian rolled his eyes.

"You heard him," Sebastian said, his voice raspy and breathless. At least he was feeling the same thing I was.

"Yes, I did," I told him. "I'm not hungry."

"I am," Sebastian replied, his eyes sliding to my mouth again. "But not for food."

"I hope you're dressed, 'cause I'm comin' in," Toby announced from the door, and I jumped off Sebastian, getting to my feet and nearly falling over.

"He's kidding." Sebastian sounded sure of himself, but I realized he'd gotten to his feet too, and he had planted his hands on my shoulders, keeping me from falling into the small desk in the corner. "Come on. Let's eat."

I nodded. I had no choice.

Once again my voice had disappeared into thin air.

As we walked into the living room, I checked to ensure that my robe was closed while hiding behind Sebastian. Not that I was worried about anyone seeing the shorts and tank top that I was sporting, but I felt a little exposed. That was the reason I used the fluffy cotton robe to cover myself because I certainly wasn't cold anymore.

Sebastian stepped out of the way and allowed me to take a seat before he did the same. No one said a word, but I heard Toby and Chloe snicker a time or two. I was halfway through one of my pancakes when I asked, "So what the hell's going on here? Did you stay the night?"

Toby's eyes widened and his smirk disappeared immediately. I guess he hadn't expected me to call him to the carpet.

I shot a sideways glance at Sebastian and smiled. At least, for the moment, we were out of the hot seat. After all, it wasn't like we were sneaking around. He hadn't stayed the night with me. But I wasn't so sure that Toby and Chloe hadn't done the horizontal mambo last night.

"No, he didn't stay the night," Chloe said, annoyed.

"No? Then why is he here?"

"Because he likes pancakes."

"Is that right?" This time Sebastian spoke, eyeing Toby across the table. "Since when?"

"Since right now," Toby answered quickly, his eyes trained on his pancakes.

"You sure?" Sebastian inquired.

He was waiting for Toby to look at him, but it was clear the man wasn't going to.

"I take it the two of you are seeing each other?" I asked Chloe when no one said anything else. She seemed just as interested in studying her pancakes as Toby.

"I'd say that's a yes." Sebastian looked at me, then lowered his voice and leaned closer. "He hates pancakes."

"I do not! These are fucking perfect," Toby growled.

Sebastian and I laughed, Chloe's face turned beet red, and Toby just watched the three of us.

Then the table erupted in laughter.

"Fine, I hate pancakes."

"You do?" Chloe asked, her eyes wide.

"Yeah."

"Then why are you eating them?" she asked.

"Because I don't think I can say no to you."

All laughter ceased immediately. My gaze bounced back and forth between Chloe and Toby. Yeah, there was something going on there for sure. I just didn't know what it was. I wanted to ask her, but I knew now wasn't the time.

Toby pushed his pancakes away and Sebastian laughed. "Told you."

Chloe reached over and smacked Toby on the arm. It wasn't hard, more like a love tap which had me joining Sebastian as we chuckled.

I'm not sure when I'd had that much fun. At least not in a long time.

"So, what's the plan for the day?" Toby asked, not talking to anyone in particular.

"I've got to go see my dad," I announced.

"You gonna take your boyfriend to meet him?" Toby joked.

"He's not my boyfriend," I blurted, although there wasn't any heat behind it. Who said boyfriend these days?

"Based on that look, I'd say you're wrong," Chloe commented.

"Whatever." I didn't look at Sebastian, but I could feel him looking at me.

Whatever was happening between us… it was hopeful. I could admit that much. The chemistry was off the charts, something I hadn't experienced with anyone in a long time. But the fact of the matter was, I worked for Mr. Trovato. I needed my job, and I didn't think it would go over well if he found out I was dating Sebastian. I still didn't know how they were related, but I knew they were. Too many coincidences and all.

"What about you? What're your plans for the day?" Toby asked Sebastian directly.

"I've got a couple of errands to run. Then… who knows."

I watched Sebastian speak, but I barely heard the words. He was so incredibly handsome. There was that bad boy vibe that I got, but it belied the way he treated me, which was surprising. I'd always thought that bad boys had a God complex, but Sebastian wasn't like that. There was an air about him. He had a quick smile, although I could see something raging in his eyes. But he certainly wasn't the cocky, arrogant type. Not all the time anyway. He had a magnetic pull on me. And likely plenty of other women, but when I was with him, I saw something else. Something deeper.

Wow. And now I was acting like I actually knew him. We still hadn't hashed out any of our personal histories and I'd only met him a week ago, yet here I was acting as though this might actually go somewhere.

I really needed to get a grip. I had too much going on at the moment and getting involved with someone who clearly could make me lose focus wasn't a good thing.

Since I wasn't the type of girl to sleep with a guy just because my hormones thought it was a good idea, I wasn't even sure whether this would continue anyway. When Sebastian looked at me, I saw heat in his gaze. And it was burning me alive. But I knew I couldn't give in to it. Not yet.

Maybe not ever.

"Okay, well…" I pushed my plate away, trying to play it cool. "I've got to take a shower. I've got things to do."

With that, I pushed to my feet and looked at the three of them.

I was just about to walk away, proud of myself for putting a little distance between me and Sebastian when he looked up and smirked. "Need help with that?"

Yes. No. Damn it. The answer was no.

"No. Thanks for the offer though," I answered, my voice choppy.

Yep, it was safe to say that I was in no way equipped to deal with a guy like Sebastian. It didn't even matter how much I tried to talk myself out of it, I knew if he continued to work his way into my life, I was going to give in.

And that was the last thing we all needed.

Chapter Twenty-Three

Payton

"Hey, kiddo!" my father greeted when I walked into Fowler Body and Frame an hour later. Several heads turned to look my way, a couple of waves followed.

"Good morning, Amy." I smiled at my father's receptionist who was sitting at a small desk near the front door.

"Mornin,' Payton," Amy replied, not looking up from her computer screen. "How's the new job?"

"Great." I didn't bother to stop and address her directly. Truth was, Amy didn't like me all that much. I knew her pleasantries were for my father's sake. Not that there was any love lost on my part. I didn't particularly care for Amy either. I thought she was a manipulative, vindictive bitch. And an attention whore.

"Hi, Daddy." My smile intensified as I approached my father.

"What're you doing here?" he asked, his surprise to see me written across his handsome, aging face.

My father was in his late fifties, but working in the body shop industry had aged him. He looked quite a bit older than that. He kept his dark hair clipped short, mainly because he was balding, and he had plenty of laugh lines around his eyes and mouth. But no matter what, he was still one of the most handsome men I'd ever know.

So I might have fibbed a little earlier when I told Sebastian that I had to go see my father. It had been the first thing that I thought of, but I knew I needed to have a plan for the day. The last thing I needed was for Sebastian to think I had been planning to sit around my apartment and hope he would call. Yeah, so, coming to see Harold Fowler wasn't really a scheduled thing, but I figured since I had told Sebastian that I had to stop in and see him, I probably should. That or my spur of the moment comment would have been a lie.

When my father wrapped his arms around me, I hugged him back. "Just wanted to stop by."

Sitting around waiting for a guy didn't really work for me. I was supposed to pretend to be only partially interested in Sebastian. Anything else would make me look desperate.

I was a little desperate.

Especially when I thought about the way he kissed me, the hard planes and angles of his body beneath my hands. I wanted to throw caution to the wind and jump him.

I was thankful for the little bit of common sense I had left.

I knew that until Sebastian opened up and told me some things about himself, I wasn't going to give in. So his inability to share about himself was my only saving grace.

"Want something to drink?" my dad offered after he released me, rubbing the top of my head like I was five.

"Sure," I replied, trying to smooth my hair back into place.

I followed my father into the small break room at the back of the building, passing two other employees who merely offered a brief wave before burying their noses in their computer screens once again.

I didn't go to my father's body shop often. Fowler Body and Frame was one of those places that made me feel out of place. The people were nice, but I knew what they saw when they looked at me. After all, even though my father had wanted me to, I never gave in to working there full time. It wasn't for me.

I enjoyed the time I spent with my parents, namely my father who had toted me around to hockey or baseball games and car shows as a kid. There was no doubt about it, I was definitely a daddy's girl. But even though I loved spending time with him, I didn't want to work for him. Aside from the few times I had filled in when Amy needed to take time off, or my stint as my father's assistant during my senior year of high school, I didn't spend a lot of time there.

Sure, I knew about cars. More so than I cared to, really. I could change my oil, fix a flat tire, and even identify certain engines based on the set up under the hood. But other than that, being at the body shop wasn't high on my list of favorite things to do.

"How're you, kiddo?" Harold, better known as Hal, asked after retrieving two cans of soda from the small, secondhand refrigerator that stood in one corner of the break room next to the sink and a long counter complete with a used microwave. On the other end of the room was a flat screen television mounted on the wall and one of those water jug machines.

"Good," I answered, pulling out one of the metal chairs and sliding down into it while I glanced around the room. "Did you paint in here?" I asked, noticing something was different.

My father surveyed the room briefly before meeting my eyes again. "Yeah." He pointed to a spot in the ceiling. "We had a water leak, ended up having to paint the whole room after they fixed it."

"I like it," I told him, unable to think of anything else to say.

"Did you watch the Stars beat the Predators the other night?" He grinned widely.

"I did. Good game."

"It was. One of these days we'll have to go see the Stars play again."

We hadn't been to a hockey game in at least two years. Mainly because of my father's busy schedule. "I'd like that."

"So, how's work? Did you meet Mr. Trovato?"

I smiled, leaning back in my chair and wrapping my fingers around the cold soda can. "It's good."

My father cocked an eyebrow, obviously waiting for me to answer the other question.

"And, yes, I met him." I laughed. "I'm his assistant."

He nodded as though he was contemplating my answer. "Have you met a lot of people?"

"Not really, no. I'm kinda isolated at the moment. I did have to go to Mr. Trovato's house last week though."

My father's eyes narrowed on me.

Oops. That probably didn't sound right, especially when I blurted it out.

"He left his cell phone at home and his wife couldn't bring it to him."

"That's a strange thing for a receptionist to be doing," he said simply.

"I'm not a receptionist, Dad. I'm an administrative assistant."

"Same thing."

I smiled. No, they weren't the same. At least not in a company the size of Trovato, Inc., but I wasn't going to argue with my dad.

"How're you?" I asked, not really wanting to talk about me.

"Good. Busy."

"Yeah?" I was a little surprised by his hurried response. There hadn't been any cars in the parking lot when I arrived. Since it was Saturday, I kind of expected them to be busier.

I also knew that things had slowed down quite a bit for my father in recent months. My mother had mentioned it one day, and I'd heard something in her tone that I hadn't heard before. Concern.

"Is there anything I can do to help?" I offered, sipping my soda.

My dad chuckled. "We're good. You should be enjoying your day off, kiddo."

I knew I should. But that meant sitting around my apartment thinking about Sebastian and that was something I wasn't comfortable with. It was bad enough that I'd woken up that morning and the first thing that had crossed my mind had been him. I didn't want to be that girl. I was twenty-three, not seventeen. I had things to do and places to go.

Liar.

Okay, so I had nothing to do on a Saturday. Shopping was out of the question because I was trying to save money. Hanging out with Chloe wasn't an option because, shortly after I mentioned needing to go see my father, I found out she had planned to spend the day with Toby. I still intended to bombard her with questions where they were concerned, but I couldn't do that until she was home. Alone.

"How's Aaron? And Chloe?" my father asked, his gaze darting out the door.

I twisted to see someone standing there, clearly waiting to talk to my dad.

"I'll be there in a minute," he told the guy before turning his attention back to me.

"They're good," I told him. "Aaron's spending most of his time with his new boyfriend. And Chloe's busy with work."

"Boyfriend, huh? I assume he's a good guy?"

My parents loved Aaron, always had. Considering we'd spent so much time together, he was practically a member of the family. In fact, my parents had helped Aaron when he had concerns over talking to his own parents about being gay.

"He's nice," I told my father honestly. "I kinda think they're spending too much time together, but I'm not a relationship expert, so what do I know."

"Have they been together long?"

"A few months."

My father nodded and, as I was looking at him, a question flitted through my head and before I knew it, I was speaking it aloud. "Do you know if Mr. Trovato has any kids?"

My dad's brows turned down and I could see that I'd taken him off guard with the question.

Explaining my reasons for wanting to know the answer to something like that would have probably been a good thing, but I kept my mouth closed. Well, actually, I pretended to take a drink of my soda until he finally answered.

"He's got a daughter, I know," my father explained hesitantly. "There'd been a rumor a while back that he had a son as well, but that had died quickly. I think he's got a nephew that lives with him."

My soda nearly came out of my nose. A son? Was Sebastian Conrad's son? It made sense. They did kind of look alike. But…

Nooo. No way was Sebastian Conrad's son. He couldn't be.

I thought back to the pictures in Conrad's office. There were several of Aaliyah growing up, including several of her in recent years. He had pictures of his wife, Lauren, on the bookshelves that lined the far wall. But other than that, he didn't have any other pictures. Certainly none of Sebastian.

Why would Conrad keep that a secret?

He wouldn't, that's all there was to it.

"Nephew, huh?" I asked when my coughing fit settled.

"Why do you ask?"

"No reason." I shrugged, placing my can on the table. "Look, I know you're busy and I've got… something to do."

My father stood when I did, concern etched on the hard lines of his face.

166

"Tell Mom I said hi," I told him as I hugged him quickly and then turned toward the door.

"Payton."

Ahh, crap.

I stopped walking and turned to face my father.

"Is something going on?" he asked quietly, his voice low.

"Nope. Not a thing. I just have to run. Talk to you later, Dad."

I couldn't wait around for him to dig deeper. I wouldn't be able to keep my thoughts to myself.

And until I heard the words from Sebastian's mouth, I didn't want to jump to conclusions.

Although, I was pretty sure I already had.

Chapter Twenty-Four

Payton

Two hours later I was pacing the floor in my living room, staring at my cell phone on the coffee table. I was disappointed that Sebastian hadn't texted or called. Granted, he thought I was busy with my father. It still bothered me that I hadn't heard from him at all.

Should I text him? Should I leave him alone? Should I pretend he doesn't exist?

Wow. The last question drew me up short.

My thoughts deviated to the conversation I'd had with my father earlier. Was it really possible that Conrad Trovato was Sebastian's father? If it were true, why didn't Sebastian just say so? And why didn't Conrad have any pictures of Sebastian in his office?

"What the hell? Who could do that to their kid?" I spoke aloud although no one was home to hear me.

The guttural roar of an engine jump-started my heart. I darted to the window, scanning the parking lot below for the car and there it was.

Sebastian's sleek black Camaro was parked next to my Mustang, and I found I couldn't move as I watched him climb out. He was so damn hot. The way he moved, the way he carried himself. All masculine grace and power. Watching him took my breath away.

Yeah, I was pretty sure he was a god sent to this planet to make women forget their own names. He was… beautiful.

Tall, with narrow hips and a broad chest. His hair always looked like he'd been running his hands through it. Today he was wearing a black leather jacket and I felt the saliva pool in my mouth.

I hadn't realized that I'd been standing there staring at him until there was a knock on my front door. I closed the distance in two steps and flung the door open, coming face to — well, not face because he was so much taller than me — chest with Sebastian.

"Hey," he greeted in that dark, sexy tone.

"Hey back. What're you doing here?" I asked stupidly. I hadn't expected to see him, especially since we hadn't made any plans that morning. I had wanted to, just hadn't expected to.

His eyebrow darted up slightly and he stared at me, his eyes narrowing. "We need to talk."

Oh, crap. I didn't like the sound of that.

Sure, we needed to talk, but did we need to *talk*?

The way he said it sounded bad.

"Come in." I stepped out of the way and motioned for him to come inside. My stomach had plummeted to my feet, and I felt a little lightheaded as I stared after him.

He was wearing jeans — no surprise there — and a body-hugging black T-shirt beneath the leather jacket and a pair of black work boots. He looked like a fallen angel with his golden brown hair, the top just a little long, and his brilliant gold eyes. The five o'clock shadow darkening his jaw made him appear rugged and even sexier than when he was clean shaven.

"Can I get you something to drink?" I asked, wanting to be the polite hostess. More importantly, I didn't want to stand there and stare at him. Only because the idea of getting caught was a little embarrassing.

"I'm good," Sebastian said, not making eye contact with me.

That bothered me.

That had been one of the first things I noticed about him. He always made eye contact. And not the simple kind where he just spared you a look. No, Sebastian's eyes practically dug into your soul. He left me feeling exposed in every way. And now he wasn't looking at me at all.

"Want to sit down?" I asked, motioning for the couch.

Sebastian nodded his head, but he didn't move.

Unsure what to do, I moved closer to him, standing directly in front of him and looking up. He didn't meet my gaze.

"Is something wrong?"

His eyes slowly slid up until they were locked with mine. I'd say something was wrong. Where I'd previously seen mischief and excitement, at the moment I saw… fear?

No. That couldn't be it.

How could this strong, brave man be afraid of anything?

"Sit down," I whispered, reaching for his hand and tugging him toward the couch.

Before he could answer, my front door flew open and in walked Chloe.

"Hey, y'all. Don't mind me. I'm just here to shower and change. I'm gonna grab some clothes and go out for…"

Chloe's string of words died on impact as she came to a stop in the middle of the living room.

"What's wrong?" I was confused by the way she was looking at Sebastian.

"You okay?" she asked Sebastian directly, not answering my question. "You look pissed."

Sebastian's head lifted, and he forced a smile. "Peachy. Just here to talk to Payton," he mumbled, his voice gruff. Chloe merely nodded and then spared me a glance before she started toward her bedroom. Before she got there, she turned back to look at me. I thought she was trying to tell me something, but I pretended not to notice. I wasn't sure what just transpired in my living room, but I didn't want to talk to her. I wanted to talk to Sebastian.

"Come on," I told Sebastian, taking his hand and leading him into my bedroom before closing the door behind us. With Chloe in the apartment, there was no way we would have any privacy sitting in the living room.

Without thinking, I climbed on the bed and sat cross-legged as I watched him.

"Sit," I instructed as I patted the comforter, feeling awkward that he was still standing.

He looked at me then at the bed before shaking his head. "Not a good idea."

Oh.

O-o-oh.

Okay.

"Then pull up a chair," I stated, clearing my throat. I hadn't thought about what it would look like if I flopped onto my bed and invited him to join me.

Sebastian shook his head again and walked back and forth in the few scant feet that were allotted him. He pulled off his leather jacket, hung it on the back of the chair, but that was the only time he stopped moving. He resumed his pacing, his eyes glued to the floor.

My apartment was small. The bedrooms were big enough to hold a queen sized bed, dresser and a small desk. Nothing more than that. And I had more than that in mine, so that left even less space to maneuver around. Considering I only used the room to sleep, it had never bothered me. With Sebastian standing there, my bedroom felt even smaller.

"You want to talk?" I felt like I was poking a stick at a scared animal. Any second now, I thought he was going to turn and run.

"Yeah." He still wasn't looking at me.

Okay, so this was getting weird fast.

"Please sit. You make me nervous when you pace the floor."

Sebastian dropped onto the edge of the bed and I couldn't believe my eyes. A minute ago he hadn't wanted to sit there for whatever reason and now… well, there he was less than a foot away.

"Is something wrong?" I asked when he didn't speak. The silence was unbearable. I was focused on the way he was breathing. Shallow and choppy.

I knew the answer to his question before he said it.

"Yeah," he muttered. "Something's wrong."

"Oh."

Well? I wanted to shake him, force him to spill it, but I thought better of it. Touching him probably wasn't a good thing right now. I could see the strain in the muscles of his neck.

Sebastian shrugged out of his jacket, setting it on the back of the chair near the bed.

That's when I saw the muscles of his arms, his bulging biceps decorated with black ink, the corded lines of his forearms, a clean slate for whatever tattoo he might want in the future.

"What is it?" I finally asked when the silence stole the oxygen from the room.

Sebastian twisted until he was looking directly at me. The heat in his eyes was potent, hot enough to scorch the surface of the sun.

"I want you, Payton."

Uh…

I wasn't sure what to say to that.

"And I shouldn't."

"Why?" Hmm… I was starting to think I sounded a little needy. If that one word hadn't come out quite so breathless and anxious, I wouldn't be worried, but I knew how it sounded.

"You work for…"

I waited. This was the moment of truth. He was going to tell me who he was. Truthfully, I knew we couldn't even attempt to go any further until he did, so I held my breath.

"Who?" I wanted him to tell me, to open up and let me in.

Sebastian was instantly on his feet, pacing the floor again. At this rate, the cheap carpet was going to have a hole in it before he was finished.

Moving closer to the edge of the bed, I reached for him when he made another pass by me. He stopped instantly, staring down at where my hand touched his.

Then slowly — ever so slowly — his eyes moved up my arm, my neck, my mouth until we were staring at one another.

"Payton, I can't explain it—"

I didn't give him a chance, I tugged on his arm and he moved closer until he was kneeling on the bed in front of me. I continued to pull him, trying to bring him closer. For a second, I thought he was going to resist but then he was hovering above me and I was pulling him even closer. Close enough that our lips touched.

The room could have exploded right then, and I wouldn't have cared. The only thing that mattered was the warmth of his body above me, the feel of his rough fingers as they gripped my chin almost forcefully. Our tongues were battling and I was trying to suck air in through my nose, but it was difficult. All of my senses were aware of him. His unique, musky scent, the way the short hairs on his head tickled my palm, the hard plane of his chest pressed against my breast.

It was safe to say that I'd never wanted anyone the way I wanted him.

Never.

And it didn't even matter that I didn't know much about him other than his name and that he was related to my boss.

Sebastian pulled back, the muscles in his arms flexing as he held himself above me. "Payton. Angel," Sebastian breathed against my lips before coming down over me and delving into my mouth once again.

If you've ever had an out of body experience, then you know what I was feeling in that moment. The stars had aligned, the planets gearing up to collide, the earth had started a backward orbit around the sun...

And I didn't care because I was meant to be right there. I was meant to be with this man. There was a little voice in my head that assured me this was what was supposed to happen.

Chapter Twenty-Five

Sebastian

My heart was racing, my skin electrically charged and I wanted more of her.

I needed more.

This woman soothed the chaos in my head. Just being near her muffled the noise that was constantly screaming through my brain.

But I couldn't have her.

Or at least I knew I shouldn't.

Somehow I managed to break the kiss, pushing myself up, holding my body above Payton's. The feel of her breasts crushed to my chest, the warmth between her thighs against my leg… it was too much.

And I didn't trust myself.

I don't know why I came. I'd been driving around for the last half hour, trying to convince myself that it was a bad idea.

I should have called Toby or Leif, asked them to get a beer or even head down to the track. But I did none of that. Then I was there, in front of Payton's apartment building, pulling my car into a parking space next to hers and I just wanted to see her.

I'd had a fight with my father.

A knock down drag out that ended badly.

"I wanted to let you know that we won't be needing you in Vegas this year," Conrad informed me when he walked into the garage where I'd been working on the McLaren, trying to pass some time before I called Payton.

"What?" I asked, standing up straight.

He was standing in the doorway between the house and the garage. He was wearing a polo and jeans, his usual weekend attire.

"You heard me," he said as he stepped into the garage and closed the door to the house. "You've got to finish the concept car, and I don't think it's a good idea for you to go this year."

"We've had this planned for months." For the last five years, I had attended the SEMA show in Vegas. Truth was, I enjoyed that trip, actually looked forward to it each year. Aaliyah had just turned twenty-one and we'd made plans to go out and celebrate. I'd invited Leif and we were going to enjoy the nightlife. It was the only time I actually looked forward to spending time with my father. For whatever reason, during the show, we didn't argue. We managed to get along for the few days we were there, even if life went right back to normal the instant we returned, I still looked forward to the show each year.

"Not going to happen this year, Sebastian. I don't think you deserve to go out there."

"Deserve?" I growled, wondering if I'd actually heard him correctly. "You don't think I deserve it? How fucking old do you think I am? Five? Oh, wait, you weren't there when I was five, so that can't be it."

"This is exactly my point," Conrad countered, his tone frustratingly calm. *"You're out of control and I can't deal with your unprofessional attitude."*

I wanted to tell him to fuck off, but I bit my tongue.

"Anyway, I've asked Payton to go. I need her there. She can keep Aaliyah company and help with the show."

I swallowed hard as realization dawned. He wasn't insisting that I stay home because he thought I was unprofessional, he didn't want me around Payton. Rather than just accepting his decision and doing what I wanted anyway, which was to go to Vegas with or without his approval, I lost my shit.

"Fuck you, Conrad. I'm not a fucking kid anymore and in case you hadn't noticed, I'm the only fucking reason your company's still making money hand over fist. I'm twenty-five years old, I make my own decisions. You don't want me there, fine. But don't expect me to work on anything for you."

"You don't have a choice," Conrad yelled. *"I fucking own you, Sebastian. You're my son. You will do what I tell you to do or you'll be out on your fucking ass."*

"Is that right?" I marched right up to him and got in his face.

"That's right. And if you don't like it, I'll take every fucking penny you've got."

The laugh that escaped me was filled with anger and disbelief. "You think so? You think you call the shots? Well, I've got news for you. I've got a few secrets of my own and if you want to have a pissing match, we'll just see who wins. Try me."

Conrad's eyes widened, but he wasn't finished. "There was a reason I tried to pay your mother off, Sebastian. I didn't need the headache. I didn't need the shit that would come with it. And I was right. I should've let the state take you. I should have just turned my back on you like everyone else."

I felt like I'd been punched in the solar plexus. I stumbled backward. Conrad had said some pretty shitty things in my life. He'd done my mother wrong and I'd heard him and his wife actually talking about her on occasion, but never had he said anything that nasty to me.

I nodded, unable to get any words to form.

"You won't be going to Vegas, Sebastian. I've already told you, I don't want you anywhere near Payton. And if you don't want to find yourself out on your ass, you'll do what you're told."

It had taken everything in my power to walk away without ripping Conrad's head from his body. Somehow I managed and I made it back to the guest house, grabbing the keys to the Camaro from the bar along with my wallet before storming out. I had needed someone to talk to, someone who would listen and not judge me. The only person I could think of was Payton, although I had no idea whether she'd be the one who wouldn't pass judgment.

I suspected she wouldn't, which was why I was there.

When Payton's cool fingers scraped the skin on my sides, I realized she was reaching for the hem of my shirt, lifting it higher, her fingers sending chills down my spine as they grazed my overheated skin.

I should have stopped her. It would have been the right thing to do, but I didn't. And when she lifted the T-shirt over my head, I held my breath, staring down into her mesmerizing hazel eyes.

She was looking at me, touching me. It wasn't easy to control myself. While she studied the black ink that decorated my arms, the tip of her finger traced over the designs.

"No tattoos on your chest," she mumbled, her hands coming to rest on my pecs.

My chest was heaving, as though I'd run a mile just to get here, my abs were tight, every muscle in my body coiled as I fought the urge to devour her. She slowly slid her fingers over my skin again, her fingernails grazing my nipples, her eyes slowly sliding up to meet mine. My breath hitched.

My cock was rigid, a painful throb between my legs that was impossible to ignore. "You're making me crazy, Angel," I whispered.

"I know."

She sounded so sure of herself. As though she knew that she was tempting the beast. There wasn't an ounce of fear in her beautiful eyes.

If she only knew, she would be terrified. If she knew the demons that lurked inside of me, she wouldn't be lying beneath me. She would be barring the door, keeping me on the other side at all times.

I was a rubber band, pulled tight, ready to snap. I wanted to touch her, to taste every delicious inch of her. And I didn't want to stop until she was screaming my name.

For a moment, I thought I could do this. I thought I could give in and take her the way I'd dreamed about. I had imagined slowly stripping her clothes from her, kissing a trail up her body, teasing, tormenting until she was begging, pleading for more. I wanted her more than my next breath. I wanted to lose myself in her for hours. "Are you sure about this?" I asked softly.

"I'm not sure about anything, Sebastian," she admitted softly.

God, she felt good. Soft against hard. She calmed me. I'd never known anything like this. For as long as I could remember, I'd had the noise in my head. The fear and the anger, it was a living, breathing thing inside of me. All of my suspicions, they took control of my thoughts until I was blinded by the rage.

I didn't know how this would end, but right then it didn't matter. I would fight through hell to have her, to keep her.

But moving too fast was a surefire way of ending this before it ever got started.

And that was the last thing I wanted.

I leaned forward, burying my face in Payton's neck, inhaling her sweet scent.

"Quit thinking so hard."

Her words pulled me from my thoughts. "I can't help it. This isn't why I came. I didn't plan for this." My words were muffled against the blanket beneath us. "God, Payton, I'm not sure I can keep my hands off you."

I didn't want to, I knew that much. I wanted to touch her.

Everywhere.

But I couldn't. Not yet.

Not after what happened earlier. Not after the falling out I'd had with Conrad, the horrible things he'd said, the things I'd said.

If I made love to Payton the way I wanted, Conrad would turn it around on me, and he would make her believe that I had done it just to defy him.

That's the way the bastard worked.

And I damn sure wasn't going to let him come between me and Payton.

I wasn't going to let anyone come between us.

So, my conscience got the best of me and I rolled off Payton, flipping onto my back next to her. Without hesitating, I pulled her to me, her head resting on my chest, her palm planted over my heart.

I slid my hand under the soft cotton of her T-shirt, finding warm, smooth skin beneath. I settled for touching her, feeling her breath against my skin.

"We need to talk." I tried to regulate my heartbeat.

Payton didn't say anything.

Part of me was surprised she allowed me to stay in her room. After all, I was the spawn of Satan. Then again, she still didn't know, because I hadn't told her. I had chickened out, which was probably the only reason she hadn't thrown me out.

But that wasn't the only secret I had.

It was just one of many.

And I needed to tell her everything. I needed to open up and share, or the chaos was going to break me. I was going to implode.

"So, talk," Payton encouraged, her fingers trailing down to my navel. I sucked in a harsh breath, willing my body under control.

I couldn't get the words out although she'd given me the perfect opening.

"I want to know everything there is to know about you," Payton said softly, her body coming closer, pressing against my side.

"I'm not sure you do."

Payton lifted her head, her beautiful green-brown eyes peering into mine. "I do."

I could almost believe her.

Almost.

But I knew the instant that she learned my story she was going to run for the hills and never look back.

I looked away, staring blankly across the room. "Conrad Trovato is my…"

I swallowed hard, trying to get the words out, but they wouldn't come.

Payton leaned in, pressing her lips gently to mine. "You can tell me anything, Sebastian."

She was saying that now. In a few minutes, I wasn't so sure she'd feel the same.

"Conrad Trovato is my father." I exhaled deeply and turned my head, meeting her gaze head on. "Conrad Trovato is also…" I swallowed again, nearly choking on the words that hung on my tongue.

"Tell me," Payton demanded softly, her eyes wide.

"I'm pretty sure he's the man responsible for—"

Before I could get the words out, the front door opened and then slammed closed, rattling the window above Payton's bed and knocking a small vase from a shelf on the wall.

Payton flew off the bed, running to the door and pulling it open.

"Aaron!" Payton yelled. "What's wrong?"

Shouting ensued and I was on my feet in two seconds flat, pulling my T-shirt on over my head before following her into the living room. I had no idea what was going on with Aaron, but I was almost tempted to thank him for the interruption.

His abrupt appearance had just stopped me from telling Payton something that I wasn't sure she was ready to hear.

Something that I wasn't sure she'd ever be ready to hear.

From the author

I really hope you enjoyed the first book in the Unhinged series. Payton and Sebastian's story came to me one day when my husband and I were driving in the car. I mentioned a plot idea to him and he told me to go for it. After writing the first book in a matter of days, I asked my daughter to read it. Her excitement and eagerness for more encouraged me to publish their story.

You can stay up to date on the additional books in this series by going to my website:
www.NicoleEdwardsAuthor.com.

If you don't want to miss any release dates, sign up for my newsletter and you'll receive the information right to your inbox on release day.

About Nicole Edwards

New York Times and *USA Today* bestselling author Nicole Edwards lives in Austin, Texas with her husband, their three kids, and four rambunctious dogs. When she's not writing about sexy alpha males, Nicole can often be found with her Kindle in hand or making an attempt to keep the dogs happy. You can find her hanging out on Facebook and interacting with her readers - even when she's supposed to be writing.

Website: www.NicoleEdwardsAuthor.com
Facebook: www.facebook.com/Author.Nicole.Edwards
Twitter: www.twitter.com/NicoleEAuthor

Nicole also writes contemporary/new adult romance as Timberlyn Scott.

More by Nicole Edwards

The Alluring Indulgence Series
Kaleb
Zane
Travis
Holidays with the Walker Brothers
Ethan
Braydon
Sawyer
Brendon

The Club Destiny Series
Conviction
Temptation
Addicted
Seduction
Infatuation
Captivated
Devotion
Perception
Entrusted

The Dead Heat Ranch Series
Boots Optional
Betting on Grace

The Devil's Bend Series
Chasing Dreams
Vanishing Dreams

Standalone Novels
A Million Tiny Pieces

Writing as Timberlyn Scott
Unhinged
Unraveling
Chaos